Dear Romance Reader,

Welcome to a world of breathtaking passion and never-ending romance.

Welcome to ***Precious Gem Romances.***

It is our pleasure to present *Precious Gem Romances,* a wonderful new line of romance books by some of America's best-loved authors. Let these thrilling historical and contemporary romances sweep you away to far-off times and places in stories that will dazzle your senses and melt your heart.

Sparkling with joy, laughter, and love, each *Precious Gem Romance* glows with all the passion and excitement you expect from the very best in romance. Offered at a great affordable price, these books are an irresistible value—and an essential addition to your romance collection. Tender love stories you will want to read again and again, *Precious Gem Romances* are books you will treasure forever.

Look for fabulous new *Precious Gem Romances* each month—available only at Wal★Mart.

Kate Duffy
Editorial Director

To Arlene —

Happy Holidays!

Kathleen Wells

'99

NEW HEIGHTS

Kathleen Wells

Zebra Books
Kensington Publishing Corp.
http://www.zebrabooks.com

ZEBRA BOOKS are published by

Kensington Publishing Corp.
850 Third Avenue
New York, NY 10022

First Printing: November, 1999
10 9 8 7 6 5 4 3 2 1

Printed in the United States of America

For my father, Delbert Lewis, the record-setting glider pilot who taught me I could do anything and be anything. Daddy, may you always soar with the angels.

And for the two mothers with whom I was blessed, Mary Florence and Molly Lewis. They each encouraged me to chase my dreams and to be the very best I could be.

Special thanks to Bruce Wellins of Adventures Out West in Colorado Springs. Thank you for introducing me to the world of hot air balloons and for answering all my questions.

CHAPTER ONE

Cigar smoke hovered against the ceiling like growing storm clouds. Jeremiah's stomach lurched, as it did every time he came into this office. He had never gotten used to the pervasive odor of tobacco, sweat, and old newsprint, but it didn't seem to bother his boss. Chuck Finwick, the editor in chief of the *Phoenix Daily,* practically lived in this room.

Bright Arizona sunlight shone through the grimy windows and silhouetted the rotund man pacing in front of Jeremiah. A threadbare vest hung open over his big belly, and the sleeves of his white shirt were rolled back to the elbows. The suit pants were worn slick and shiny, Jeremiah noticed. In fact, all that seemed to be missing were sleeve garters and a celluloid eyeshade. Although the *Daily* was produced on computer like any other modern newspaper, Chuck seemed to take pride in dressing like a character from an old black and white movie about hardbitten reporters.

Even the office looked like a set. Rows and rows

of books and stacks of newspapers filled the shelves that lined the walls. Framed journalism awards hung on the few spaces in between, and Chuck straightened one carefully before turning to Jeremiah.

"J.D. Have a seat." Chuck waited and watched as Jeremiah sank into a battered leather chair. "I need you to interview a pilot for me."

"A pilot?" Jeremiah's tone sounded uneasy, even to him.

The older man nodded and flicked ashes into an overflowing ashtray. "She's getting ready to try a record-setting flight."

Jeremiah didn't want to hear anymore. Yet, through the buzz in his ears, his boss's baritone voice droned on.

Jeremiah interrupted. "What kind of flight?"

"Balloon."

"As in hot air?"

"That's right."

"And the record?" he asked around the constriction in his throat.

"Altitude. She wants to go way up this time."

Jeremiah felt a faint wave of dizziness. He shook his head to clear it.

"Would you mind sending someone else, Chuck? I'm still on another story."

"Forget it. It's not as important."

"You said it was important when you assigned it," Jeremiah pointed out.

"Perhaps I didn't make myself clear. This is an assignment. I need you to stay with this woman from start to finish. From her practice flights to her final landing."

Jeremiah forced himself to stay calm. "But—"

"I need to know what makes her tick. Why does she need this additional record? What makes her risk her life for the Guinness Book?"

Jeremiah groaned. *Great, just great.* Chuck wanted him to risk his life as well.

The editor in chief stopped pacing and nonchalantly picked up a paperweight from the stacks on his desk. He turned it in his hands as though he hadn't a care in the world. "I didn't ask if you wanted this story. I told you, it's yours."

Sweat gathered on Jeremiah's forehead. Damn and double damn, he thought. "Look, I'm closing in on my consumer scam investigation. Have Dave do this one." He slapped his knees, and started to rise.

His boss raised one hand, stopping Jeremiah's attempt to leave. "He's free, but he isn't as good as you. This story needs a real wordsmith. That's you, not Dave."

Dread overrode the small swell of pride brought by Chuck's words. Jeremiah had worked long and hard to gain this man's respect. Finwick was one of the best newspapermen in the business.

Jeremiah shifted uneasily as Chuck studied him for a long moment. "You have a problem with this story." It was a statement, not a question. "What is it?"

He looked straight into Chuck's dark eyes. "I can't do this assignment. Don't ask me to."

A vivid memory flashed through his mind. He

remembered standing at the edge of the building . . . then falling, grabbing, and missing. Jeremiah closed his eyes and shook his head to erase the image. He bolted to his feet. "Get someone else. As a favor to me."

"Tell me what the problem is, and I'll consider it."

Jeremiah stepped closer to Chuck, their noses inches apart. The younger man's jaw was set, his fists clenched at his sides. "Just send Dave."

Chuck seemed to consider the demand, then shook his head. "Sorry. It's yours." His voice dropped to a little above a whisper, and he shrugged his massive shoulders. "Or you're fired."

Amelia walked to the door of her oversized garage and looked skyward. She slid one hand into a hip pocket of her jeans, leaned against the doorjamb and watched. At least twenty silent gliders, piloted by young cadets, circled on air thermals to soar above the Air Force Academy. She understood their love of flying, their determination to be where, in all likelihood, God never intended man to be. Small planes continually took off, towing more gliders into the air as others landed. Amelia wished she had been able to launch today, but there was too much to do.

She returned to her task, walking through the large building, clipboard in hand. Amelia double-checked pieces of equipment, marking them off one by one. This wouldn't be her first attempt to set a record, but just like the others, her excitement was growing as the challenge drew near.

The shrill ring of a phone screeched above the sound of an oldies station playing on the radio. Amelia turned the volume down to a reasonable level and snatched the offending instrument off the wall. "Hello."

"Amelia?"

She sighed when she recognized the voice of her sponsor. What did the woman want now? "Hi, Carrie. What's up?"

"Can't I call to just say hello?" Carrie sounded hurt. Amelia didn't buy it. As shrewd in business as she was soft, round and grandmotherly, Carrie always got what she wanted.

"Sure—sorry. How are you?" Amelia waited, knowing she probably wouldn't like what was coming.

"We have the most wonderful opportunity to publicize your flight, dear."

Amelia groaned, but Carrie went on, not hearing or not caring, Amelia couldn't be sure. After all, this was what sponsors wanted when they put their money on the line.

"The *Phoenix Daily* is sending a reporter to do a whole series of articles on you and this flight." Amelia heard the sound of shuffling papers and waited, knowing Carrie would continue in her own time. "Name's Jeremiah something. He's going to cover all the preparation and practice, right through the final flight." Her excitement lilted through the phone line.

"Why the *Phoenix Daily*? Why not a local paper?"

"The editor in chief is a friend of mine, and I advertise heavily in the Phoenix area. Since I have a division of the company there, he agreed to do this for me."

"Carrie, a reporter on special assignment will just get in my way. The regular guys are enough of a problem." Amelia twisted the phone cord around her fingers. "We need this to be a successful try. I don't need that kind of distraction."

Carrie harrumphed the way she always did when she wasn't getting everything her way. "Well, I could get Lindsey to do the flying for me." She hesitated and Amelia pictured her patting her blue-gray hair, the cunning look of a predator shining in the older woman's eyes. "You won't even agree to fly with my logo. Most other pilots do, you know."

"This flight is my attempt to match or break my grandmother's record. You agreed I could use her balloon with the plane on it, and that I could put your logo in a different place." Amelia squeezed her eyes shut against the dull ache in her forehead.

"I know, but we still need coverage. That's what I'm paying for. Besides, you want people to know about Edith, don't you?" Carrie hesitated, then found the right button to push. "You're very proud of your grandmother and want to share that, right?"

The silence grew heavy, and Amelia gave in. "All right. Send him over. I'll talk to him."

"Thank you, Amelia. He'll arrive tomorrow." Amelia heard the "gotcha" in Carrie's voice. "Put him somewhere, will you? You're a dear."

The line went dead before she could reply. Amelia gently placed the receiver on the holder.

She shook her head. There was no denying her sponsor had lots of money and clout, but she could be a real pain. Carrie was right, though, Amelia admitted to herself. She did want the world to know of her grandmother's accomplishments; she just hated having to draw attention to herself in order to do it.

Sweat dripped down Amelia's neck. Storm clouds were rolling in, and the humidity was high. Just more aggravation she didn't need.

Amelia impatiently pushed an errant lock of blond hair away from her face, tucking it behind one ear. She'd deal with the problem of the reporter later. She shoved her pencil behind the other ear, bent down, and shifted a box to read the label on another.

Every flight meant planning and preparation, the boring part she hated. She was always eager to be up in the air, away from all worldly constraints, but her success and safety depended on the preflight checks. So she left nothing to the complete care of others. Amelia followed up on every detail personally before each flight.

A breath of fresh air drifted to her in the heavy warmth of the interior and enticed her away from the equipment. She walked to the open double doors, studying the towering clouds billowing over the Rockies. Amelia glanced at her watch. Only ten o'clock, and the day was already deteriorating. The thermals were just what glider pilots prayed for, but they didn't do her a bit of good.

The mountain weather was notoriously unpredictable. She wondered if an early winter would prevent her flight. She had already postponed her flight until this fall, although it meant gambling on thunderstorms and early snow, banking on the colder weather to help her attain greater heights. Nonetheless, she would still need time to get up and out of range before the seasonal storms could build to the deadly level that had killed her grandmother. And she had to be able to land safely.

Her carefully planned launch would require several hours of good flying time and that could be a rare commodity in the Rockies at this time of year. The aspens had turned gold, their leaves clinging to the limbs in a final holdout against winter. When the sun went down, so did the temperature. It was hard to believe on a hot, sticky day like this, but she knew that winter was definitely on the way.

She wiped her dirty, damp palms over tight jeans. The weather could be a problem, but it wouldn't be the first delay she ever experienced. She wanted this flight done, though. This one was special; she felt it in her heart. She intended to reach new heights.

The air conditioning chilled Jeremiah to the bone when he walked into his apartment. His shirt clung to his back, thanks to the blazing heat of the Phoenix sun. Which was just the kind of weather he liked. Hot. The hotter the better.

Jeremiah stalked to his bedroom, his friend and colleague at the *Phoenix Daily* close on his heels.

"Hey, man, what's up? You headin' out?" Dave asked.

Jeremiah barely looked at him. "Yep. Gotta go to Colorado." He pulled drawers open, grabbed clothes and threw them into a suitcase.

Dave shrugged. "What's the hurry? Hot news flash? How come Chuck didn't call me, too?"

"It's more of a human interest piece than news, if you ask me," Jeremiah grumbled. "I get to chase some female pilot around for the next week or two." He threw another clean shirt onto the pile.

His friend raised one eyebrow. "A pilot?"

"Uh-huh."

"You have to fly with her?"

"Yes. In a hot-air balloon, no less."

"Are you nuts?" Dave shook his head.

Jeremiah glared at him over the lid of his open suitcase. "You have a problem with that?"

Dave raised his hands in surrender. "Nope, I thought you might."

Jeremiah clenched his jaw and dropped onto the bed. "I do. Chuck wouldn't listen to me. I tried to persuade him to assign you."

Anticipation lit Dave's eyes. "I'll call him. I love the Rockies. And females." He puffed up his chest and wiggled his eyebrows, but Jeremiah simply scowled at his antics.

"Get your mind out of the gutter. Calling Chuck won't help." Jeremiah shook his head. "His mind is made up. I practically begged him to let you do it. He wants me."

"Oh. . ."

"Dave, you and I just write differently. He thinks my style is more suitable for this one for some reason."

"Does he know about you and heights?"

"No." Jeremiah ran his hands through his hair, roughing up the waves.

Dave turned a chair around and straddled it. "Why the hell didn't you tell him?"

"Right," he snorted. "Tell my boss his award-winning, hotshot journalist is afraid of heights."

Dave shrugged. "It's not that you're afraid, exactly."

"Well, whatever you call it, I don't want to be there." Jeremiah hesitated. "Damn! I'm not walking away from another job because of this . . . ridiculous phobia. Which means I better go now, or I won't go at all." He jumped to his feet. "I'll be in touch."

He crammed the clothes into the suitcase, forced the latches closed before picking it up, and walked out the door cussing Chuck Finwick.

A film of road dust covered his vintage convertible MG when Jeremiah pulled up to the pilot's place the next day. The long gravel driveway stopped at the back door, since the house faced away from the street to take advantage of a mountain view.

He parked in front of a huge garage, adobe brown with deep green details. It blended well with the surrounding prairie grasses and terrain. Not bad, he thought admiringly. Not bad at all.

Jeremiah stepped from his sports car and threw his

Phoenix Suns cap into the back. He walked toward the huge open door, glancing around for any signs of life. The darkness inside stopped him. He pulled his sunglasses off and slipped them onto the top of his head, waiting for his eyes to adjust. When they did, he got his first look at Amelia Edith Dedham.

At least he assumed this was his target. A woman with her back to him bent over a toolbox set on a low stool. She rummaged through it, apparently looking for a particular tool. Faded jeans hugged her hips and legs, and he noticed that she wore white tennis shoes. All the better to dance in. Her hips rocked in time to the music blasting across the room. When she straightened, she tucked her hair behind her ear, softly whistling a rock-and-roll oldie.

Jeremiah enjoyed the view, but figured he'd better make his presence known. He opened his mouth to speak, but never got the chance to say anything.

The woman turned and shrieked, then swore as she dropped a wrench from her hand. It clanged on the cement floor. She grabbed it, holding it like a weapon, ready to defend herself if she needed to. He raised his hands in surrender.

Jeremiah smiled. She was the cutest pilot he'd ever seen. Maybe this assignment wasn't going to be so bad after all. "I'm sorry I startled you. Ms. Dedham?"

"Who are you?"

"Jeremiah Beach, from the *Phoenix Daily.*" He shook his head. "I guess you didn't hear me." He raised his voice a notch. "The music is kind of—"

Amelia leaned across a workbench to turn down the radio. "Sorry. I like it old and loud."

He looked her over, noted her flaxen hair and sea green eyes. Was that determination or bravery that raised her chin a notch? "It's a pleasure to meet you, Ms. Dedham." He stuck out his hand, a smile spreading over his face. Flight or not, this pilot was turning out to be a very pleasant surprise.

She glanced at his hand, then her own. Wiping it down one thigh, she reached out and accepted his. "Call me Amelia. We don't stand on formality around here."

He felt the strength in her hand in spite of her slender, feminine fingers. She tipped her head back and looked into his face. Her understated and unadorned beauty made his groin tighten, and desire coursed through his body. Jeremiah recorded every detail in his mind's eye. He wouldn't forget her soon, even if he wanted desperately to forget what they would be doing together in the coming days.

Amelia tugged her hand out of his grasp.

"You made good time. They only told me yesterday you were coming."

"When a newspaper editor gives you an assignment, you pack and run. That's the name of the game."

"Can I get you something to drink or do you want a tour of the place? Do you need to rest or something?" she stammered.

The tension came back to his stomach with a vengeance when he thought of her occupation. Jeremiah forced his fear aside. It was not going to cause trouble. He was determined to ignore it and concentrate on meeting his deadline.

"For starters, why don't you show me what we're going to be flying in?"

Her smile spread from delicious lips to sparkling eyes. She really loves this, he thought. Go figure.

Amelia turned and led him to the back part of the building which housed a trailer. Painted on its side was a sky blue balloon with a World War II bomber emblazoned across the side. The name Edith, written in gold script, adorned the nose of the painted plane.

She slid the trailer doors open and stepped aside. Jeremiah leaned closer to get a better look, stunned into silence. An oversized picnic basket rested inside. He felt the blood drain from his face and turned slowly to gaze into her eyes. He gulped down sheer terror.

"We're going up several thousand feet in that? With nothing between us and the ground but air?"

Amelia looked at him, a quizzical expression on her face. "Sure. What's wrong with that?"

"Nothing," he managed to say. "Nothing at all, if you're a bird," he muttered.

What a way to deal with his phobia. But his pride wouldn't allow him to chicken out. Jeremiah touched the woven wicker sides of the gondola, and rattled the edge, testing for strength. When the basket shifted in the trailer, he groaned. Jeremiah straightened up and pulled himself together. No way was this lovely woman ever going to know how afraid he was of heights.

Pride goeth before a fall. He heard it as clearly as if his grandmother were standing next to him.

Yeah, a 15,000-foot free fall, he said to himself.

What had Chuck gotten him into?

CHAPTER TWO

Amelia's gaze moved up the stranger's lean, long body, over his snug jeans and tight-fitting T-shirt to his face. His musky scent drifted to her, tickling her senses. The sight of him stirred up more feelings than it should, but it was the expression on the reporter's face that struck her. The man obviously had no clue how wonderful it was up there, floating with the wind, taking advantage of the currents to go where you wanted. At least most of the time. A soft smile spread across her face, lifting the corners of her mouth. She enjoyed introducing people to the sport she loved.

"Jeremiah, it's really great. You'll like it. Honest."

His hazel eyes drew her attention, as terror seemed to spark from them. Deep furrows creased his forehead between dark eyebrows. No one could miss his concern.

A few incoherent words escaped from his lips as he tried to reply. He ran agitated fingers through his thick brown hair. His obvious dread of the impending flight touched her.

"I'm guessing you've never been up in a hot air balloon before."

"That's right." His gaze slid back to the gondola bearing the logo of Amelia's sponsor.

"It's wonderful up there." She saw him shudder. "Are you afraid of heights, or flying in general? Or do you get air sick?" She noticed that his gaze remained locked on the wicker basket. "Because that's not usually a problem in a balloon," she finished.

Finally, he managed to get a few words out. He faced her. "I'm not afraid to fly. I love it. Do it all the time to get to assignments."

She decided it was best to ignore his words. This man was obviously not telling the truth. Whatever his reasons, Jeremiah didn't want to fly with her, and he wasn't ready to tell her the reason why.

Amelia led him away from the trailer and into her office. "How about a soda?" She opened a small refrigerator and surveyed its contents as Jeremiah wandered about the room. She popped the top on a can of soda without waiting for an answer and handed it to him, taking an orange Nehi for herself.

Trophies and photos lined the oak-paneled walls. Jeremiah drank absentmindedly as he looked them over, halting in front of a picture of an old World War II B-52. She watched as he looked at the photo, then at her and back at it. As it always did, longing tugged deep at her heart. The picture never failed to stir up emotions she thought were best left buried.

Amelia pushed down her feelings and smiled. "That's my grandmother. She was one of the first women to ferry planes to Europe for the army. A lot of people don't even realize women did that."

"There's a striking resemblance."

She nodded. "So I've been told."

"Isn't this the plane painted on your trailer?"

"That's right."

"Edith," he read from the photo. "Your middle name."

"You've done your homework."

"That's my job." He shrugged. "You were named for her," he added.

"Is this where you start taking notes or something?" she asked, growing uncomfortable.

"No." He shook his head and smiled.

She hadn't noticed his dimples before. How had she missed those? Her gaze slid to his eyes. Amelia's heart stuttered like a bad piston. Get a grip, she scolded herself silently. Still, he was good to look at. This could be fun. She forced her attention away from him and back to the subject.

"I was actually named for my grandmother and Amelia Earhart. Grandma was named for the first woman to fly." Amelia chuckled. "Some people think I take risks going after balloon records, but Edith Berg went up with Wilbur Wright in one of his contraptions."

"So that's how you got tagged with Amelia Edith."

Amelia grimaced. "Dad said I had to be a great flyer. It was a self-fulfilling prophecy." She slipped her hands into her hip pockets. "Let's talk about flying. That's much more interesting than me."

"You're part of the story." He shrugged. "People will want to know what makes you tick."

She felt the heat of a blush slowly rise up her throat to her cheeks. "Why should anybody care about me?"

"Well . . . " He thought for a moment. "You're doing what you dreamed of doing your whole life. You don't turn away from a challenge." He cocked his head to the side. "That takes courage. So I have to find out what drives you, where you get that determination."

Amelia set her soda down on the desk, staring straight into those eyes of his. "You're here to cover this flight. Don't psychoanalyze me." She saw his jaw tighten, and realized she'd been too sharp. "Sorry. I'm just a private person. That's part of why I like it up there, alone."

"You're a celebrity. People are interested." He downed the last of his drink. "Why don't you tell me where to find a hotel, and we'll call it a day? We can start fresh in the morning."

Disappointment warred with Amelia's common sense. She should be glad he was leaving. Why wasn't she?

"There's a decent place a couple miles from here. I'll point you in the right direction."

"Thanks. Are you doing a practice run tomorrow?"

Amelia nodded.

"What time?"

Her spirits lifted as they always did when she thought of a launch. "Five a.m."

"Five," he squawked. "You're kidding, right?"

"Haven't you seen balloons launch?"

"I don't get up that early unless I'm covering a military coup or earthquake." A frown creased his forehead; the dimples were gone from his tanned cheeks.

"When do you write? I thought reporters liked to get cracking on a story before anyone else."

"Not me. I work best between ten in the evening and four in the morning."

"That's the middle of the night." She laughed with him.

They were obviously appalled by each other's work schedules. "Five a.m.," she repeated. "And don't be late, or you'll miss the flight. I don't wait for anybody."

Amelia pointed at him and touched his chest with her fingertip. "Be there. You'll love it."

Heat seared from his body and into hers. She drew back as though burned. She glanced at his face, then quickly away. Was that a mutual attraction she saw briefly reflected in the depths of his eyes? Amelia quickly discounted the thought, but couldn't help wondering what it was going to be like trapped in the small gondola with a man this handsome every morning for the next week.

Jeremiah arrived at the launch site before the sun. After writing until well after midnight, he'd caught just a few hours of sleep before his wake-up call came from the front desk.

He dragged his body from the car, a styrofoam cup

of coffee from the local stop-and-rob clutched in his fingers. Silence surrounded him. So did the mountain cold of an early day. He pulled his collar up around his ears, sipped the bitter coffee, and burned his tongue.

Swearing, he wished he knew where the hell everyone was. He reached into the car and pulled out the directions he'd been given the night before. Jeremiah skimmed them, recalling each turn he'd made. Yep, he was in the right place. But where the devil was Amelia?

Something stirred deep within when he thought of the slim blonde. Not that she was petite or anything, but compared to his height, she was pretty small. One meeting and he could picture Amelia as clearly as someone he'd known his whole life. Could see the smile always hinting at the corners of her mouth and the sparks flying from the green depths of her eyes whenever she talked about flying.

Jeremiah rubbed a hand over his smooth chin. He had shaved at three-thirty this morning. He must be crazy. He should have just crawled out of bed. But he hadn't been able to keep himself from shaving and using his cologne, or from pulling on a clean shirt. He told himself it was so he'd be presentable if he ended up dead. And he had to admit, he wanted to make a good impression on Amelia.

His wandering thoughts screeched to a halt as a sudden rain shower pelted down. What next? He slid into the car and slammed the door. The weak overhead light allowed him to see his watch. Five-thirty.

The sun wasn't even peeking through the light clouds still obscuring most of the sky.

"Where the hell is she?" he muttered.

Grabbing his cell phone and notebook, he punched in her number. The phone rang a dozen times before a sleepy voice answered.

"What?" the woman said.

"Amelia?"

"Yeah. Who is it?"

"Jeremiah!" He fought to control his temper. Mornings were not his thing. Freezing his butt off this early in the day was definitely not his idea of a good time. "Where the heck are you?"

Silence.

"Amelia!"

"Didn't you get my message from the hotel?"

"What message?"

"Flight's canceled, bad weather. Go back to bed."

The phone went dead. Jeremiah rested his head on the steering wheel, cursing Chuck Finwick, the weather, balloons, Amelia Dedham, and the world in general.

He pictured her tucked away safe and warm in her bed, the covers pulled up to her chin. The image was anything but unpleasant. What did she sleep in? he wondered. Forget just wishing he was warm and in bed, what would it be like to be with her?

As if she'd want a man who's afraid of heights. With a disgusted sigh, he started the car and headed back to bed, cold, wet, and lonesome. Going to her place and finding her alone, snuggled in a warm bed, would not be a good idea, he concluded. They needed to stay on a professional level and he was beginning to think that wouldn't be easy.

He'd talk to her about her lapse in communication after he got a few more hours of sleep. It wouldn't do to tear into her for leaving him stranded at this ungodly hour.

Amelia was setting her lunch dishes in the sink when she heard the car stop outside. She walked out the back door and saw the sleepy-eyed reporter, and felt her heart beat faster. Why, oh why, did her body react to Jeremiah Beach so strongly?

The screen slapped shut behind her as she greeted him. "Good morning." She glanced at her watch. "Or should I say good afternoon?"

Jeremiah scowled at her.

"You look like you need caffeine. Name your poison—coffee or soda?"

"While you were warm and snug in your bed, I was waiting at the park."

Amelia saw the sparks in his eyes, temper or something else. It didn't matter what it was, her breath hitched.

"Rule number one of ballooning, always check the last-minute weather reports and see if you have a go or not. Rain means no go."

"You could have warned me." He sounded like a disappointed little boy.

"I'm sorry. It didn't occur to me you wouldn't know

to do that. I did call the hotel and leave a message for you."

"They didn't have someone giving out messages at that hour," he said.

She walked into her garage, with him following. "So how did you sleep?" she asked teasingly.

"Just peachy, both times. So what's the game plan for today?"

"I'm going to spread out the envelope while I have time."

He looked puzzled.

"The balloon itself is called an envelope. I'm just going to check it out."

"What for?"

"On days like this, when I don't fly, I always go over the balloon to be sure there aren't any weak points or tears." She saw concern in his eyes and stopped short of adding she'd rather find them before a launch and not after.

"Come on. Let's get you some caffeine, and I'll show you."

Amelia tugged on his hand to start him moving toward the office. His strong, warm fingers closed over hers for just a moment before he pulled away. The contact was brief, but pleasurable—at least to her. She turned a startled look at the man beside her. He walked on, seemingly oblivious to her reaction.

Damn, Jeremiah thought. A good reporter knew better than to get involved. Stay objective, he reminded himself. If he was going to react to her every time she touched him, they were in trouble. Had she felt the electricity between them? Maybe it was only his problem.

He had to focus on this story. "So, tell me. How many records do you hold?"

Amelia smiled at him. "I thought you did your homework."

"I did. The latest reports I could find showed eleven. That right?"

She nodded, blond hair swinging loose around her face. "Yep. This one will make an even dozen."

"Will that be enough?"

"Of course not." She stopped walking and turned to him. "Don't you ever do a story from a fresh angle just because it's never been done that way?"

"I guess I do. I hadn't thought of it like that." Jeremiah considered her comment. "I like to be the first, on the leading edge, so to speak."

She turned and ducked into the office, coming back with a soda. She shoved it into his hand and walked on toward the balloon trailer. "So do I. That's why I have to fly higher, farther, whatever. I'm not satisfied with doing what everyone else does."

Jeremiah thought of the practice flights, rubbed the dull ache in his right elbow. "Do you always do all these practice runs Chuck told me about?"

"Not really. But I signed a contract to test experimental equipment on this trip. I want to be sure the instruments are recording accurately before I count on them."

He grabbed her arm, and they jerked to a halt. "This is a test flight? Like. . . " He struggled for an image. "Like that old Jimmy Stewart movie? Flying things that don't have a right to stay in the sky?"

"Not at all." Amelia chuckled. "Do I look crazy?"

Jeremiah gazed into her face, gave the idea serious consideration. "No, I guess not."

"I've flown this balloon hundreds of hours. The only things new are the flight instruments. It's new equipment I'm testing for a large balloon company." She shrugged. "Nothing to worry about. I do it all the time."

"You may, but I don't."

"Look, Jeremiah, when are you going to level with me about being terrified?"

"I'm not—" He stopped, looked at her raised eyebrow. "All right, I am. But I do what I have to do, just like you do." He had psyched himself up to be in the air this morning, hadn't he?

"If it helps, lots of people are scared silly the first time."

"It's not that simple."

"Why don't you tell me about it? Maybe I can help," she said softly.

He rubbed his elbow a second time. "I don't think so. I don't want to go into it. I'll be fine." Jeremiah realized he was rambling and snapped his mouth shut.

"Look." She lifted her hand toward his arm, then dropped it to her side. "This is serious business for me. I can't have you freaking out up there."

"I told you. I do what needs doing."

A flicker of concern shadowed her eyes. "So do I, and I don't want anyone flying with me hurt."

"How many tests flights do we have to do?"

"Four or five."

Jeremiah groaned.

Amelia smiled reassuringly. "You'll love it, I promise."

Jeremiah's heart thudded in his chest. "I hope so. I really do."

His gut twisted into knots, but this time he wasn't sure if it was the thought of flying or the good-looking blonde beside him. Jeremiah had interviewed hundreds of people, but never anyone quite like her. What a package Amelia was—intelligent, gorgeous, and brave. In his mind, you couldn't beat a combination like that.

They were going to get to know each other better. He'd make sure of that. After this assignment was done, he'd thank Chuck for sending him to write about Amelia Dedham, right before he killed him for making him fly in a balloon.

CHAPTER THREE

Jeremiah wished for rain. It didn't work. It was a perfect day to launch, or so he'd been told. Light reflected along the horizon in the cloudless morning sky. The day would be clear—and hot, by Colorado standards.

At the entrance to Memorial Park, flags flew at half-mast in tribute to military veterans. A winding road led around green slopes and recreational areas. Cottonwood and oak trees reached for the sky, their leaves turning the delicate gold of early autumn. The gold contrasted with deep green pines, punctuated by tall blue spruces. A handful of early risers jogged along the road.

Jeremiah pulled into a parking spot and turned the ignition off, gazing through the windshield at the silhouettes of three people. Two stood on either side of the outstretched balloon, and Amelia operated a roaring fan that was slowly filling it. The balloon raised partially off the ground, then slumped down. Just like he felt, limp and ineffective.

Get out of the damned car, you coward, he told himself.

One foot hit the pavement. Jeremiah hesitated, the other foot still where it could reach the gas pedal. He didn't want to leave the steel sanctuary. He did it anyway, gently closing the car door, not wanting the noise to offend the gods of balloning or whoever he was going to pray to up in the air. Jeremiah figured he'd need all the help he could get this morning.

He sipped his coffee and swallowed it as easily as rocks. He dumped the dregs on the pavement, then rolled the empty cup between his cold fingers before tossing it in a trash can. He shoved sweaty hands into his jacket pockets and walked toward the others, hoping this wouldn't be his last day on earth.

An ironic chuckle escaped him. He was praying to stay alive, but getting ready to head into the sky in a damned picnic basket.

He watched the threesome work, taking in the sights and sounds. The ambiance of the chill morning air, the sounds of the crew hustling around the fanned-out balloon, calling out instructions to each other, the sight of Amelia directing the whole enterprise, filled his senses. All of it was crucial to his story.

A slim, dark haired woman in frayed jeans and a patched jacket worked beside a blond Adonis in designer jeans and a leather jacket. Adonis had a cheerful smile on his face, in contrast to the serious concentration of the woman. An unusual crew, he thought. Jeremiah decided to interview them later, to get more background on Amelia and the kind of people she surrounded herself with.

Jeremiah slipped his cold hands into the pockets of his coat. It was hard to believe it would hit eighty degrees, with dew-damp grass beneath his feet and a chill in the air. At least in Phoenix the weather was predictable. Around here you just waited a few minutes and it changed.

Amelia spotted him and waved. "Morning." Her voice wavered above the noise of the fan. "How are you doing?"

"Great. Just great." He forced the coffee burn in his stomach from his thoughts. "Can I help?"

"Sure. Get on the other side and help guide the balloon as it fills. Debbie and Paul will show you what to do."

She looked him up and down. The hair on the back of his neck rose. He didn't like being analyzed, and it was clear that was what she was doing.

"Are you going to be all right?" she asked.

He sucked in cool air, filled his lungs and exhaled in an audible whistle. "Yeah. I'll be fine." He rubbed his elbow through his lightweight jacket. Cool weather always made it hurt. That and memories, he admitted to himself. He dropped his hand and went to help the crew.

In minutes the balloon filled and floated above the gondola. The sky blue envelope towered above them, her grandmother's bomber logo appearing to fly just above their heads. What would happen if the balloon got a big rip in it? Could it do that? Beads of sweat popped out on his forehead, ran down his cheeks and quickly chilled.

He looked at Amelia as she waved him forward. Jeremiah strode to the basket with all the confidence he could muster. He fought to keep his heart from exploding as it threatened to do at any moment. His blood pressure must be over the top. Jeremiah had his own B-52s, and they were doing dives in his belly.

"Okay, now listen up," she said. "When we come back down, we have two options for landings. The first is no wind and a nice, easy set down. All you have to do is hold on to the handles and bend your knees like a skier to absorb the impact." Amelia demonstrated for him.

She hesitated for only a second. Long enough to worry him.

"And the second?" he asked.

"No big deal, but if it's breezy, I'll tell you to get down. Then you brace your back against the basket in the direction we're coming in, and hang on until we land and stop moving." She smiled reassuringly.

"Chuck Finwick is a dead man," Jeremiah grumbled. "Right. I can do that."

"Okay then, sit on the edge and swing your legs over," Amelia directed him. He half crawled and half fell in beside her, making a graceless entrance to the gondola.

She grabbed his arm and steadied him as the heavy basket tipped slightly on the uneven ground. His back braced against the wicker side, Jeremiah grabbed the edges in a tight-fisted grasp.

A camera dangled from his neck, and his pockets bulged with extra film. A notebook and pen were tucked in his inside coat pocket. He doubted his hands would be steady enough to use any of it, or that he would let go long enough to try.

Jeremiah watched in horrified fascination as Amelia blasted the burner. Fierce heat flashed across his face in the cool morning air, and the fine hairs on his neck singed. The roar subsided as she let off the controls, then grew in a crescendo as she repeatedly rekindled the flame.

They rose, pulling the guidelines from the crew's hands. Jeremiah wanted to yell at them to hold on. The balloon drifted free, rising above the park. He closed his eyes tight, wishing it all away. His breath came in short gasps as his pulse jumped and raced. Jeremiah's gut twisted again. He feared he was going to humiliate himself by losing his breakfast in front of Amelia.

Her touch on his arm startled him, and he opened his eyes. Amelia gave him a thumbs-up sign. Jeremiah raised one brow and sent her a weak smile. Thoughts raced through his mind. He'd covered devastating fires and earthquakes, rebellions and wars, all on the front lines. He'd been on the run from guerrillas and had hidden from drug dealers. Jeremiah wasn't afraid of anything else. Why couldn't he get over a simple thing like a fear of heights?

The balloon skimmed the tops of buildings and trees, then quickly rose several thousand feet. Amelia pointed out the huge, red rock formation known as the Kissing Camels in the Garden of the Gods. Manitou Springs nestled in the foothills as they floated along the slope of the Rocky Mountains.

"Why don't you get some pictures of those historic buildings from here? I bet they'd be great shots."

Jeremiah heard her words, but didn't move since his hands remained attached to the basket. His mind had been working overtime, but he hadn't uttered a word since the flight began.

"Maybe talking about it will help you get over your nervousness," she suggested.

He silently shook his head.

"Step away from the side. I'll show you the equipment."

Amelia reached over and pried the fingers of one of his hands from the gondola. He refused to budge, wondering how solid the floor between him and oblivion actually was. She tugged until he moved closer.

She blasted the burner again, then let the silence settle over them. There was no sensation of movement, no sound, no breeze. Jeremiah realized they simply were part of the universe, moving within the confines of time and space.

"Jeremiah?"

The noise of another blast drew him back. "Just taking it all in."

"Good. That's a start." Amelia explained the equipment, and he focused on the workings of the balloon.

"It's really sophisticated," he said at last.

"You bet. You're as safe here as in that jet you mentioned."

He gave a half-hearted laugh. ''I don't know about that, but I can see you know what you're doing.''

''Balloon pilots don't have a death wish, Jeremiah.''

''Could have fooled me.''

He glanced around, careful to look up at clouds and sky. Pike's Peak loomed in front of him as the balloon continued south. Clouds were beginning to stack on the mountain summits. He wondered what happened to these things in a thunderstorm. What would a lightning strike do?

''What happens in bad weather?'' He had to know.

''Nothing, because we always check the weather and don't go up if it's iffy.''

''Surely you push it sometimes. I read about that attempt to circumnavigate the globe. They ended in the drink because of bad weather.''

Amelia sighed. ''That's true. Sometimes people gamble on the outcome in order to get the record.''

The hair rose on the back of his neck as his heart rate picked up speed. He sucked in a deep breath, forced himself to refocus on her.

The scent of rose petals teased him. From Amelia? He wasn't sure. Sunlight bounced off the short, sassy cut of her hair. His gut twisted again, but this time not from fear. From anticipation. How well could he get to know her during their time together?

Jeremiah forced his attention back to his job. He needed to record every bit of this, every sensation, every thought, every fear. Chuck expected him to put his readers in a balloon with their feet propped up in a favorite recliner. He'd want them to feel the heat of the flame, to feel what it was like to be airborne.

Between blasts of the burner, the trumpet of an elephant mingled with the sound of laughing children drifted to them from the Cheyenne Mountain Zoo. Jeremiah didn't look to see if the children pointed skyward at the balloon, he just assumed they did. He knew they would be enthralled by the balloon.

"Well, what do you think?" she asked.

"It's . . . " He swallowed a lump, tried again. "It's awesome."

"Told you that you'd like it."

"I wouldn't go that far. But I might survive this assignment." He felt the dimples he hated deepen as he smiled. "I think."

"Good." She grinned. "Glad you're at least getting used to it." She looked over the side.

"Look at that." Amelia pointed to a small herd of deer racing over the hills below them.

Jeremiah followed her gaze. Then he quickly jerked his eyes level with hers, and felt the blood drain from his face. "Oh, man, that was a mistake." He clamped a hand over his heart.

"I'm sorry. I wasn't thinking." She reached toward him, but dropped her hand.

"I forgot where I was."

Jeremiah didn't do edges, or heights. Here she was trying to achieve a new altitude, and all he wanted was to stay firmly planted on the ground.

He listened to Amelia radio her ground crew. Hope spread like wildfire, lifting the heavy weight that had been his heart before it turned to stone. "We're going down now?"

"That's right."

"How long have we been up here?" he asked.

Amelia glanced at her watch. "Oh, an hour and a half I guess. I didn't pay attention to the exact launch time."

Jeremiah chuckled. "Feels like three days."

He watched her peer over the side.

"There they are." Amelia pointed at the crew, but this time Jeremiah didn't look.

Their chase truck and trailer moved along the highway below them, guessing which way the wind would carry the balloon. Jeremiah hoped they'd be waiting to help with the landing.

As they lowered over the treetops and power lines, Jeremiah couldn't decide whether he wanted the balloon to get higher or if he should grab a passing tree and get the heck out of the basket. A tall pine jutted above a grove and the basket scraped the top of it, shimmied and then steadied again. Jeremiah scooted carefully to the side and clutched the edge. He kept his gaze locked on Amelia, wishing fervently they were already on the ground.

She smiled as they drifted, then concentrated on the landing. Jeremiah risked a glance over the side as the trees got closer. The ground moved toward them, but not as fast as he'd expected. He'd anticipated the feeling of falling, of seeing the ground rising up to meet him at a deadly pace. That didn't happen. They simply floated down as though being set on earth by unseen hands.

Amelia recognized his anxiety. "It's not too windy. Good landing today, Plan A, gentle set down." She met his gaze with a steady one of her own and a warm, reassuring smile.

He nodded and swallowed the new lump in his throat. There seemed to be a basket full of softballs lodged there lately. Jeremiah wanted desperately to be back on terra firma, but was leery of the landing itself even though Amelia was the picture of confidence and ability. Using the vents, she rotated the balloon and brought them down between a fence and the power lines that followed the road.

The gondola hit the ground, skidded and came to rest with a thump. Jeremiah tightened his grip. Amelia ripped open the vent to deflate the balloon. As it sank to earth, the balloon dragged the basket over, tumbling Jeremiah out before he could hop over the edge. Paul and Debbie rushed to help, capturing the balloon and stretching it into a huge roll to pack.

Jeremiah fought the urge to kiss the grass. Instead he clutched the long blades in his fingers and thanked his lucky stars for putting him back on solid ground. Jeremiah stood and locked his knees to stay upright, swaying slightly. Vertigo made his head reel. After a few deep breaths, his head cleared, and his stomach settled down.

Amelia and her crew loaded the balloon and gondola into the trailer faster than he would have thought possible. Then she walked to Jeremiah, and he grabbed her and swung her off the ground. He stopped spinning around before he got dizzy again and planted a quick kiss on her lips. Slowly, he set her down, letting her body slide down the front of his.

Amelia stiffened, shock registering on her face. He put his hands on her cheeks, circled his thumb over one high cheekbone, and looked deep into her eyes. His lips captured hers in one more gentle kiss.

Need pulsed through him at the warm contact of his mouth on hers and jolted him back to reality. He dropped his hands and stepped back. Her eyes glistened and her face flushed to a delicate pink. He was relieved that she didn't appear angry at his behavior, only surprised.

"What was that for?" A crooked grin curved her lips. "Didn't you think I'd get you down in one piece?"

He refrained from dancing a little jig. Jeremiah didn't want Amelia to think he'd completely lost his mind. "I need to get my impressions down on paper. There's something to this ballooning thing," he said. "Thanks." He turned away, but she grabbed his sleeve.

"Going up with me tomorrow?"

His lungs deflated faster than the balloon and sank into a lump in the pit of his stomach. Indecision hit him right between the eyes. Ballooning reminded him of riding a rollercoaster as a kid. The ride had always scared him, but he'd race off the thing and run to the end of the line to go again. The terror had been fascinating and this flight affected him the same way. It had been one of the most exhilarating experiences of his lifc, but fear sat firmly at the edge of his mind.

A weight settled in his chest. "Yes. I have to."

"Maybe this assignment will help you."

"I don't know, Amelia." He sighed, a deep and weary sound.

"Tell me about it."

"No." He shook his head and grabbed the notebook from his pocket. "I'll catch up with you at your place. How about I take you out for dinner?"

"I don't know if that's a good idea."

He was disappointed by her sudden refusal, but he pushed the feeling aside. "Strictly business. I need more background information for the story." He hit the button he knew would work. "You can tell me more about the flying."

"All right, but why don't I cook something easy at the house and show you a Colorado sunset from the verandah?"

"Sounds like a plan."

She hesitated, then added, "There's a hot tub if you want to bring a swimsuit."

Jeremiah suddenly pictured Amelia in a skimpy two-piece and nearly choked. He nodded. "Sounds great. Thanks."

He watched her hurry to the truck. Strength and confidence radiated in every step. What a woman. Lost in his thoughts, he turned away from her as she opened the door.

"Jeremiah?"

He snapped out of it. "Yeah?"

"Aren't you forgetting something?" she asked as he faced her. A quirky grin curved her full lips.

Jeremiah could think of lots of things he should forget. Was she thinking the same? "What?"

"Are you hitchhiking to your car or would you like a ride?"

An embarrassed heat crept up the back of his neck. Jeremiah slapped the notebook closed and headed toward the truck. "I'll take a ride."

CHAPTER FOUR

Jeremiah climbed out of the car, taking a bottle of wine with him. Once again, he admired the way Amelia's adobe house harmoinzed with its natural setting, plains that ran to the base of the mountains. Dried grasses surrounded the house's broad verandahs and rustled in the evening breeze. Flower beds overflowed with bushes of orange and yellow marigolds. The house faced a fantastic view of Pike's Peak dusted with snow.

Amelia leaned out the back door. "Come on in. I'm in the kitchen."

The porch light haloed her hair, turning it brilliant gold. A welcoming smile lifted the corners of her lips as she disappeared back inside.

Need, hot and strong, swept through him. He wondered for the hundredth time if coming here was a good idea. Stay objective, his reporter's common sense reminded him. Don't get involved with the people in your stories.

This was a big mistake, but, oh, what a mistake!

He smiled and headed for the house, whistling softly. Let things go where they would. The cigar-smoking image of his editor, Chuck Finwick, giving advice popped into his head. "Objectivity makes for good reporting." Jeremiah's steps slowed as he frowned, until he heard Amelia's voice singing slightly off key to an old fifties ballad. *Screw you, Chuck.* Some temptations were too strong to resist. Why should Jeremiah fight nature?

The screen opened on silent hinges. He pushed it wide and stepped into the red-tiled room. Amelia stood at the sink. The room could have been a cave. All he saw was her. His gaze traveled from her soft blond hair all the way down her long legs. She looked cool and collected in beige linen slacks and an emerald green blouse, with its sleeves rolled up to the elbows. The lovely shape of her derriere in the elegantly tailored slacks made him feel anything but cool. Jeremiah dragged his gaze from her body to the back of her head.

Amelia looked over her shoulder and smiled. "Hi. What have you got?"

"Champagne. I thought today deserved a celebration. Where are your glasses?"

She shut off the water and reached for a dishtowel. "The champagne flutes are over there." She nodded toward a heavy antique sideboard. "I'll get the *aperitivos,* and we can sit on the patio. I promised you a Colorado sunset."

He noticed the dining room table set for two and gave her a quizzical look.

"When the sun goes down, we'll want to come in here. The temperature will fall hard and fast."

He shivered. "Good plan."

"You must really prefer heat to live in Phoenix," she said.

"That's right. You see, I have this theory. If I were supposed to live in cold weather, I'd have been born with fur or feathers. Since I wasn't, I figure that means I'm supposed to live in a warm climate."

"Warm? A hundred and ten plus?" She grinned at him.

"Relatively speaking, that is."

"Well, I'll take cool. Besides, it's hard to ski on sand." She laughed at his mock shudder. "Come on out."

Jeremiah followed her, his gaze drifting to the soft sway of her hips. Something stirred, threatened to bring his body to life. He forced his attention to opening the bottle of chilled champagne as she arranged trays of food on a low table.

Warm fingertips settled on his arm. Jeremiah looked at her, a question on his lips. She put her finger to her mouth, signaling him to stay quiet and nodded toward the grassland in the near distance. He followed her gaze.

A half dozen antelope grazed fifty yards from the house. One doe had new twins at her side. Jeremiah smiled at the wonder on Amelia's face. She must have witnessed this same scene often, yet she looked as though she were seeing it for the first time. They watched in silence until the small herd moved on.

"Those babies were late in the season. Hope they make it through the winter." Amelia frowned for a moment, then turned her gaze to Jeremiah.

He unwired the cork and worked it loose, laughing as it popped and flew into the air. The champagne bubbled over, and Amelia shoved the crystal glasses under the liquid fountain. He put the bottle down and stared into her eyes. She seemed to wait expectantly.

He clinked his glass to hers. "Here's to living and breathing and being alive to write this story. Thank you for keeping me that way." He sipped, looking at her as he did. "Today was great," he added quietly.

"You're quite welcome." Amelia lifted her glass to her lips and did the same, smiling at him over the rim. "I would have thought you'd view me as your personal torturer, not as a savior."

"Well,"—he grinned—"that, too. But who knows? Maybe I'm into torture?"

Amelia choked on her champagne. "I don't think we'll go there."

She pointed to a lounge chair, and he dropped onto it as she took the one next to him. For several minutes before she broke the silence, they enjoyed the quiet evening while munching on the appetizers she'd prepared. Amelia plucked a tiny *taquito* from the tray and dipped it in her homemade guacamole.

"Sorry about the food."

He raised one eyebrow in a what's-wrong-with-it look.

"This stuff goes with margaritas, not champagne."

"The cuisine is delicious," he said in a serious voice. "Impertinent but approachable. Spicy but not too." His voice took on a pompous tone, and he lifted his nose in the air. The twinkle in his eye gave him away, and she laughed.

"Truly, this is quite a spread. You're an excellent cook," he said. "I'm used to eating junk food or out of cans."

She sent him an apologetic smile. "I don't entertain often, so when I do I enjoy really going all out. I thought you might enjoy Mexican food since it's so popular in Arizona. I hope you don't care that it isn't seriously spicy. I don't do heat—of any kind."

He didn't seem to know quite how to respond to that statement, and Amelia shifted in her seat.

"So tell me, what did you think of the flight?"

He laughed. "I've given that some serious thought today. You know, to get it down on paper."

"What did you decide?" She tucked loose hair behind her ear, and he noticed her colorful earrings. A minature hot air balloon floated below each lobe.

He was immediately tempted to kiss her pretty ear and her throat and below.

"Well?"

Jeremiah jerked his attention back to her question. "It was wild. I've never experienced anything like it. It was a kaleidoscope. Elation, adventure, thrills, sheer unadulterated terror." He shook his head, sipped wine. "I didn't think I'd live through it. I'm not sure I want to do it again, but I have to."

"Jeremiah, I still think it would help if we talk about

what's bothering you. They say sharing things like this is the first step to getting over them."

He let out a deep sigh. He didn't want to talk about it at all, ever, but maybe she was right. Perhaps it was time, and she seemed to want to understand.

"It was a long time ago. I was a reporter on the high school paper." He smiled at her sheepishly. "Always wanted to write." He fell silent.

"And. . ."

"And I was at a dance. I did all of the reporting from sports to social events to important news breaks. Stories like *Who Stole the Team Mascot?* flashed across the headlines with my name under them."

Amelia laughed.

"It always gave me a thrill to see that byline—Jeremiah Beach." He gave an exaggerated sigh of sheer ecstasy.

"I understand that. When the ballooning records are updated, I love seeing my name on a new one."

"You got it." He rolled his glass between his palms.

"So you like to write and you were on a story. And. . ."

"Anyway, I was at the school dance. A young girl caught her boyfriend in the back of the gym with another girl. She was devastated and ran to the top of the building." He shook his head in disbelief. "She meant to jump."

"I can't believe she'd kill herself because of something like that."

"Unfortunately, she was really shy and felt humiliated by it. Her best friends had seen it, too. A crowd gathered and I saw what was happening, so I went up with a couple of the other kids to get her down."

"Oh, no. Don't tell me she did it."

"Well, actually, she did, but I caught her hand. I managed to get her up and one of the other guys grabbed her." He stopped, drifted back in thought. The silence grew heavy.

"Surely that wasn't enough to create this kind of fear."

He shook his head. "You're right. I was trying to pull her all the way up. I leaned over to grab her legs." He fought the vivid memory and pushed it aside so he could speak of it. "I lost my balance and fell."

Amelia gasped and slapped her hand over her mouth. Her eyes were huge. She slowly lowered her hand to her lap.

"How far?"

Jeremiah rubbed absently at his elbow. "Oh, I don't know. The school was modeled after a Spanish mission, so it had a bell tower. I fell off it and hit a convertible parked in the lot. The top cushioned my fall." He gave a short laugh. "Guess that's why I drive one—loyalty."

"How badly were you hurt?"

"Physically? A crushed elbow, broken leg, crushed vertebrae, and one heck of a concussion. The doctors said I was real lucky. Psychologically? I haven't been able to look over an edge or get up anywhere really high since."

"What about the girl?" Amelia asked.

"She made it. I understand she got some counseling and married a nice guy a few years after graduation." He stretched his legs out, crossed them at the ankles.

"Didn't your boss know this before he sent you here?"

"He had heard something about it from a colleague of mine, and my guess is he knew about my fear of heights."

Anger sparked in her eyes. "How could he assign you to cover my flight? What an unkind thing to do."

"We've worked together and been friends for a long time." Jeremiah smiled, surprised that he was defending Chuck. "I think he was trying to get me over it."

He saw the compassion reflected in her eyes, saw the fact she was ready to fight for him. No one had gone to bat for him in a long time. The strength of her concern spread over him like sun-warmed honey. The need to hold this woman surged into Jeremiah's heart. He forced it aside.

"Let's forget it for now. I'm starved." He picked up his glass. "What's for dinner?"

Amelia slid the last plate into the dishwasher and closed the door. She had refused Jeremiah's offer to help, preferring to have him relax, sitting with his chair balanced on the two back legs. The small fire she'd built in the kitchen's beehive fireplace took the chill off the room and he seemed to be enjoying it. When she glanced at him, he smiled.

"What?" she asked.

"Just thinking you sure do look domesticated for a daredevil pilot."

"I'm not a daredevil." She scoffed at the idea.

"You don't call setting altitude records risky?"

"Sure, but I don't go about it like that. I think of daredevils as the pilots who were barnstormers, flying machines that they kept in the sky with a wad of chewing gum. I'm too careful and methodical for that."

"That's good to know."

Amelia shook her head and let the silence slide over them as she dried her hands on the embroidered towel. His gaze followed her around the kitchen in a companionable and comforting caress.

Just his presence made her realize something had been missing from her life. Someone, she corrected herself. Someone to share evenings like this one. How long had she been lonely and not even realized it?

When she glanced at him, a smile curved his lips and those heavenly dimples reappeared. Her heart did a little dance as her toes curled from the look in his eyes.

"Just what are you looking at, Mr. Reporter?"

"I cannot tell a lie," he said. "You. I'm looking at you and enjoying the scenery. Immensely. Do you mind?"

"No, I don't think I do." Heat raced up her throat and over cheeks Amelia knew would turn red. "What do you see?" Her voice was husky.

Jeremiah rose, crossing the room to stand in front

of her. He cupped her flushed face. Amelia laid her hands over his, felt the warmth in his long fingers. Her lips parted in anticipation of his kiss. A soft, gentle kiss that left her lips tingling and her heart racing. A kiss that left her wanting more. She pulled his hands away and stepped back.

"I, ah, I think we'd better use the hot tub if we're going to. It's getting late. You can change in the bathroom over there. I'll meet you on the verandah."

Small lights glowed around the edge of the patio. The sky looked like heavy blue velvet, sprinkled with millions of tiny, glittering diamonds. Cool, clean air blew down off the Rockies and across Amelia's face.

She was already soaking in the heavenly bubbles of the jacuzzi when Jeremiah walked from the house to join her. She laughed at his shocked expression when his near naked body felt the shock of the chilly night air. Amelia called out for him to be careful as he ran toward the hot tub.

Amelia watched him and noted he looked even taller in a brief swimsuit. A suit that left little to the imagination and fit snugly over his trim hips. Solid thighs and shapely calves hinted at the jogging she thought he must do to stay in shape. Her gaze took in his muscle-ridged chest, following the dark line of hair that tapered down his flat belly to disappear beneath royal blue lycra.

She glanced toward the mountains, now hidden in the darkness. Amelia took a sip of iced mineral water, trying to cool her body, hoping she could cool her thoughts as well.

"Hey, you started without me," Jeremiah teased as he slipped into the hot water, settling an arm's length away.

"I told you. I don't wait for anyone." She smiled and reached for a tray on the ledge next to her. "Champagne or mineral water?"

"Water, thanks."

She turned to a wooden table set against the side of the deep blue tub. An assortment of drinks and an ice bucket rested there. Amelia squeezed lime juice into chilled water, then dropped fresh slices and cubes of ice into the crystal glass before handing it to Jeremiah.

"I thought you just didn't wait for people to launch."

She shook her head. "Nope. When I'm ready to go, I go. Doesn't matter what I'm doing. My folks always thought I was a little too independent, but I always blamed them." She grinned in the dim light. "After all, it's their fault, they raised me."

"You said they encouraged your flying. How?"

"Do you ever stop asking questions?"

His gaze captured hers, unblinking. "Only when I've learned all I want to know about a . . . subject."

The pleasure of his company made her feel warm all over, but she wondered just how much she wanted Jeremiah to know about her. How much could he learn in just a few days?

"Well," he prompted. "Your parents, flying?"

"Dad created a monster." Amelia chuckled. "He taught me to fly when I was ten."

"Ten! Isn't that too young?"

"It's too young for a license, but he let me fly when we went up together if we didn't have passengers." Her eyes got a little moist. Amelia cursed her soft heart. "He convinced me I could be anything, do anything," she said.

"What else did he teach you?"

"Oh, I don't know. Precision, perhaps. If you're going to do something, do it right." She imitated her father's voice. "That sort of thing. And not to let anyone tell you that you can't achieve your dreams."

"Sounds like you have a good relationship."

Amelia smiled into the night. "Oh, yes. I'm very lucky that way. I really like both my parents."

"Will they be here for your flight?"

"You couldn't keep them away. Especially since this one's in memory of my grandmother," she added quietly. "Fair's fair. That's enough about me." Amelia clinked her glass with his and leaned back against the tub. "Tell me about the life and times of one Jeremiah Beach. I never knew anyone named Beach before."

"Actually, it wasn't always Beach. It was Beachy."

She raised one eyebrow. "You changed your name?"

"My dad did. He was Amish but he didn't want to be. Jumped the fence, as he called it." Jeremiah shrugged. "When he went into the modern world, he wanted a name he felt was stronger, more worldly.

Mind you, he was a kid when he did it, but he had it legally changed."

"Jeremiah. That's from the Bible, isn't it?"

"Yep. And old-fashioned."

"Well, I like it. I think it's a strong name, full of integrity." She stopped, embarrassed by her revelation.

Why on earth did she say such things to a man she barely knew? And why had she let him kiss her? She sighed and slipped deeper into the foaming water, wishing she'd learn to keep her impulsive mouth shut and her thoughts to herself.

"Did your parents write like you?" Amelia asked, trying to change the subject.

Jeremiah laughed. "Not really. Dad left the community but not the lifestyle. He farmed in the midwest for years. I think that's why I headed to a place where the sun shines more than three hundred days a year. Too many gray days back there."

"And your mother?"

"Now, she is a poet." He sighed. "She loves to write poems about nature, spirituality. Whatever moves her. Only problem with having a writer as a parent is that all the time she's telling me how wonderful my stuff is, she's editing it." He chuckled and sipped from the glass he held, then slipped it onto the rim of the hot tub.

"Where are they now?"

"Still on the farm in northern Indiana."

A peaceful silence filled the night air between them. The fall moon rose above the plains, luminous and huge, appearing simply to hang in the sky. Amelia had moved out of arm's reach of Jeremiah, so she stretched and touched his thigh with her foot. He jumped, lifting his gaze to her face. She nodded toward the moon.

"Beautiful, isn't it?"

"Yes, gorgeous."

He wasn't looking at the moon.

"The moon," she whispered.

That particular heavenly body was the last thing on Jeremiah's mind. He continued to study her. She shifted uncomfortably, set her glass on the ledge of the hot tub.

"Maybe we'd better call it a night," she said.

"I'd rather not." He reached for her, and slid her across the pool and into his arms.

Amelia floated against his chest as his arm enclosed her ribs. A breath apart, he held her and moved one hand slowly up her leg to rest on her hip. He dropped a light kiss below her earlobe, tasting the sweetness of her skin.

She shook her head. "Not a good idea."

"I know," he whispered.

His lips claimed hers, then, in a hot kiss filled with longing. Her heart skipped a beat, then raced from sheer desire. Amelia slipped her hands around his neck, sliding her fingers into his hair, and pulled him closer.

Jeremiah sighed. "I've wanted to do that from the first moment I saw you fishing around in that toolbox."

"You did, after the flight."

"That was different. That was gratitude."

"So what's this, lust?"

"Uh-uh. This is different."

She laughed, her lips still close to his. "How many ways to kiss are there?"

"Lots. I'll show you, but I'm serious. I've never known a woman as independent and determined as you. You intrigue me."

She kissed his forehead, his eyelids, and his nose as she urged him close again. "Do you like strong women, Jeremiah? Women who sometimes take the lead?"

His answer was lost in their kiss. Her mouth opened to his probing tongue as their lips melted together. Jeremiah's mouth was chilled from his iced drink, but quickly heated.

Need shimmered through her body. The masculine scent of his cologne mixed with that of the cedar tub and grassy plains. Jeremiah slid his hand around her bare waist, pulling her body close. Pure pleasure filled the core of her being, threatening to spiral beyond control. Where she sat across his lap, she felt the evidence of his desire. The pulsing need in his body snapped her back into focus. She didn't have time for complications, especially sexual ones.

Amelia pulled away and dragged in a calming breath of cool air. "I think we'd better not do this."

He held on to her, but she pushed against his shoulder.

"Jeremiah, stop. I have to stay focused on this flight

until I set a new record, and you have a story to write. Am I correct in assuming you need to stay objective to cover this story the way your boss would want it?"

A heavy sigh slipped from Jeremiah. "Yeah, you're right. I hate that." He grinned at her, albeit reluctantly. "Can we do this again later?" He wiggled his eyebrows at her, making her laugh.

"Let's make a deal. After the record is in the bag, I'll take you on a very special champagne breakfast flight," she said.

"I wouldn't think you'd mix flying with booze."

"Of course not. But I can land in a nice, high mountain meadow, and it will take the crew a while to get to us. That's where we'll have our champagne breakfast."

"That sounds like the kind of flight that could make me forget how far up we go. You're on."

Amelia smiled.

CHAPTER FIVE

An annoying and persistent beep pierced Amelia's subconscious. She fought her way out from under the dusty-rose quilted comforter that covered her and slapped the top of the offending alarm. The digital readout provided the only light in the room; everything else was deep in the shadows of pre-dawn. Three-thirty a.m. Amelia groaned.

She burrowed down and covered her head with a fluffy aqua pillow. The snuggle lasted only a few moments, as she remembered today's launch and energy coursed through her sluggish body. She pushed aside the blankets and swung her feet to the cold tiled floor. Amelia gasped and slid her slippers over to rest her feet on.

Leaning over, she quickly shut the window against the crisp night air. The atmosphere carried a hint of dampness. Disappointment threatened to devil her once again.

Grabbing the bedside phone, Amelia hit the auto dial to the national weather service. The recording droned on for a couple of minutes. It reported the information she needed but didn't want. Fog and early morning rain. *Oh, shoot.* Her shoulders sagged. There'd be no flight today.

She grabbed the pad with the hotel phone number on it and punched in the number for Jeremiah's room. The phone rang just once.

"Beach," came the barked response.

"Jeremiah, I'm canceling the launch. I'll check in with you later." She dropped the phone on the stand. Amelia saw no reason to waste words at this hour.

She crawled under the covers and drifted into a light and restless sleep. Colors blended, then separated to become clear. Purple and gold flames rose at the edge of her mind. From the flames rose a figure. Amelia stood at the edge of a cliff and peered into the distance. Then she fell, spiraling down into a bottomless pit. Her heart flew into her throat.

In a black void, air rushed past her cheeks, whipping her hair around her face. She screamed, her arms flailing as she tried to stop her descent.

She bolted upright in a flash of terror. Her heart jumped, thumping against her ribs. Sweat ran down her chest and between her breasts, gluing her silk pajamas to her skin.

Amelia shook herself fully awake and sank against the pillows. She raised a shaking hand to her face, then dropped her hand to the blankets. *My God, was this what Jeremiah had felt when he'd fallen? No wonder he was terrified of heights.* Amelia clutched the blankets under her chin, knuckles white. The man's face floated in front of her, sheer terror reflected on his features just as it had been during their first flight. His fear twisted a knife in her chest as surely as if the pain were her own.

Amelia had to help Jeremiah. She threw the blankets aside and swung her feet to the floor a second time. Reaching for a bathrobe and slippers, Amelia flicked on the light.

She intended to get to the bottom of this and put his fear to rest once and for all. A plan took shape in her mind. Maybe he'd get closer, relax a bit, if she gave him more information about her personal background. Amelia hesitated. Did she want to reveal more about herself to someone she still didn't know very well?

A vision of his face, the brow furrowed, his lips tight, slipped into her mind. "Nuts," she grumbled. How could she not help? Amelia tucked her flyaway hair behind one ear, then slammed her fist into the mattress.

With sudden determination, she sprang to her feet and headed to the shower. She had work to do. Wasn't there a way to desensitize people who were afraid to fly?

Jeremiah drifted in a gentle dream. A beautiful woman with short blond hair and sea green eyes beckoned him to follow her. A dress as light as sea foam did little to hide her shape. He smiled softly and did as he was bid. Walking behind the small woman, he enjoyed the sway of her hips, the length of slim calves.

Blood coursed through his body and pooled in his loins.

He reached out a hand, caught her arm and swung her into an embrace. His lips claimed hers in a searing kiss. Her lips and tongue melted into his. The scent of her skin reminded him of rose petals. The feel of her hands on his chest turned him to liquid fire.

Jeremiah ran his open palms over her back, downward until he cupped her chiffon covered bottom to pull her close against the length of his hard body. Her moist lips trailed across his jaw, then down to pause over the pulse that pounded at the base of his throat. The tip of her tongue teased the beating flesh. Jeremiah found her mouth again and probed deeper, unable to get enough of her taste. His breath labored, groin throbbing, he wanted only to be lost in this woman forever. . . .

A loud ring jerked Jeremiah awake. Maybe he could ignore it. A second ring ripped through the quiet room. He snatched up the receiver. "Hello," he snapped.

"Hi, Jeremiah, this is Amelia. Are you up? Hope I didn't wake you. What are you doing?"

He heard her take a breath. "No, I'm not up and yes, you woke me, and I wasn't doing anything but sleeping." He slammed the receiver down and prayed to recover the blond goddess of his dreams.

The phone rang again. He grabbed the offending instrument from the nightstand. "What!"

"Boy, you're a grouch when you wake up."

He heard the laughter in her voice and contemplated an interesting revenge, involving silk scarves and Amelia in nothing at all. Or he could simply throw her out of one of her balloons, but then he'd be left alone up there. He shuddered and the pleasurably erotic memory of his dream ebbed away.

"What do you want, Amelia?"

"I'm taking you sightseeing."

"Sightseeing?"

"Yep."

"I thought the weather was bad," he grumbled.

"Bad enough to keep us on the ground, but that's all. I'll come get you."

"What time is it?"

He heard Amelia fumbling around and waited.

"Seven thirty."

He choked back a curse. "We don't have to fly and you're waking me up at daybreak?"

"It's not daybreak. The day's half gone. Get ready and I'll take you to breakfast in half an hour. Bye."

The phone went dead in his hand. He groaned, glared at it as though it had a life of its own and slammed it down. Half an hour. Blast. He rolled slowly from the bed and dragged his still throbbing body to a cold shower. He knew several better ways to wake up than alone in a hotel room in a cold shower, but it would have to do for now.

Jeremiah walked from the lobby and out to the curb as Amelia pulled up in her truck. The balloon logo on the side panel gave him the creeps. He didn't want to think about the next flight and the one after that and the one . . .

He told himself mentally to shut up and reached for the door handle as the truck stopped. "Morning." Jeremiah practically growled the greeting. Setting his camera bag on the floor, he crawled in.

"Hi. How are you?" Amelia asked. "It's a great day, isn't it?"

Jeremiah frowned at her. "It's a lousy day. Threatening to rain and you can't fly, so what makes you so perky?"

"We can't go up, but that gives us a chance to look around and we can talk about flying." She hesitated and he saw the frown that flickered briefly around her lips. "I'll even let you ask me more personal questions for background if you need it." She glanced at him, sent a warm smile in his direction, then returned her attention to the traffic gathering on Academy Boulevard.

The curve of her lips reminded him of something, someone. Great, he thought. Now I'm daydreaming about her. And about things I'd like to do to her. Swell.

Suspicion taunted him. "What makes you suddenly so helpful?"

"Nothing. I just thought you might like to get out of the hotel for a while."

"Uh-huh, so what's the plan for today?" he asked.

"We can eat breakfast and then hit the usual tourist places. Okay with you?"

She said it too casually to suit him. He didn't trust her for a minute.

"You know you weren't thrilled to be saddled with a reporter. Now you're playing tour guide. What are you up to, Amelia?"

She turned guileless green eyes toward him. "Up to?"

"I think you have a plan. I'd like to know what you're about to lead me into."

"I don't know what you mean. You said you wanted to learn more about the locale, that's all." She shrugged. "Won't that help put your readers in the proper frame? I'm going to take you to some of my favorite places."

Suspicion filled him, followed quickly by a flash of unease. "We can't fly today, right? Not a balloon or glider or anything?"

"No. We can't. We're staying on the ground for the whole day. Honest."

Jeremiah sighed and relaxed. "Okay then."

A soft smile brightened Amelia's face. His gut tightened as he wished he could take her in his arms and devour her mouth before moving on to the rest of her. The feeling didn't last. Concern as he studied her expression pushed desire aside.

"You have something up your sleeve." He looked her over, trying to figure out what she had in mind. With a quick shake of his head, he gave up. "I'm yours. Take me wherever you like."

Heated color spread from beneath the neckline of her jacket, across her long slim neck and over lightly tanned cheeks. He could only guess at how she had taken his comment in such a way as to bring on a virginal blush. His body stirred yet again, and he forced his libido to behave itself. Otherwise this was going to be a very long day.

With a quick breakfast behind them, they were back in the truck and driving down a winding two-lane road. Lining both sides, gigantic red stone formations rose in stark contrast to the snow-covered Rockies behind them. Hikers and bicyclists moved along trails between the boulders. They came to a flat rock face that reached toward heaven, towering several hundred feet into the air. Crawling up the surface like ants at a picnic were three climbers. They clung to the damp sandstone, pulling their bodies upward hand over hand, sliding their feet back and forth to find footholds.

"Damn fools," Jeremiah muttered. His scrambled eggs sat heavy in his stomach, the grease from sausage adding a queasy feeling to the mix.

Amelia's gaze followed his to the climbers. "They climb here all the time. That's the Tower of Babel. I'm always kind of surprised the authorities let them do it."

"And I'm amazed they want to." Jeremiah turned away from the fools hanging by their fingertips and focused on her. "So where are we headed first?"

"Right here." Amelia pulled the truck into a spot at the visitor's center at the Garden of the Gods. "This is a great place to get an overview of the

Garden. They tell about the history inside if you're interested. Might give you a little information on the area if you need it." She slid from the vehicle. "Bring your camera, there are some great photo ops from the deck."

Jeremiah's gaze followed hers to the pinkish adobe and aqua tiled building. The front of it was glass and surrounded by a deck with mounted telescopes.

They walked up the steps that curved around the building as Amelia gave him a rundown on the early ranchers and inhabitants of the park.

"You sound like a real tour guide."

"I enjoy history." Amelia smiled. "Besides, I spent my high school summers working as a tour guide to pay my flying expenses."

"Ah, another piece of the puzzle," he said.

"Come on. I'll show you where you can take photos." She led him around the front of the building instead of into it. "It's gorgeous, isn't it?"

He stared at her, and the red rock and snow-covered mountains behind her in the distance. A gentle breeze lifted her hair and something put a sparkle in her eyes. "Magnificent."

Amelia laughed self-consciously. "The scenery." She nodded across the road to the sign announcing the entrance to the Garden. "It's beautiful, isn't it?"

Jeremiah forced his gaze to follow her own. It was an unusual place.

"You know, I've been all around the world in my work. I've seen a lot, but I've never seen anything quite like this," he said.

A break in the clouds allowed the sun to spotlight the rock formations, accentuating their glorious reds and throwing the surrounding shadowed mountains into deep purple relief. It was as if God himself had illuminated the spectacular vista.

"If you looked up inspiration in the dictionary, surely there'd be a picture like this." He cleared his throat, suddenly embarrassed. "This tops most of the natural wonders I've seen, though."

Nor in his wanderings had he ever seen a woman as lovely as Amelia was, inside and out. She possessed an understated elegance and natural, unadorned beauty that just about melted him. Her presence tugged at him until he looked back at her. She appeared to study his features.

"What are you thinking about?" he asked.

"Just watching. It's always fun to show a place you know well to someone who hasn't seen it before. It's like seeing it for the first time all over again if you watch how they react to it." She pulled her jacket close against the still cool air. "Kind of makes it new." She grabbed his free hand. "Come on over here and shoot some pictures."

"Only if you let me take some of you for the story."

Amelia frowned. "Okay, but only a few. I brought you to see the area, not me."

"And I came to see the area . . . and you."

Jeremiah set his bag down and pulled out a camera. "Step over to the wall and let me get some shots of you with that big rock behind . . ." He had been looking through the lens and lowered the camera to smile at her. "That's the Kissing Camels formation you told me about in the balloon, isn't it?"

She glanced over her shoulder, then at him. "That's it. I didn't think you heard a thing I said during that flight." A warm smile tweaked her lips. "It really does look like two camels smooching."

"Sure does," he grumbled. Why did everything they did today have to remind him of what he'd like to be doing to her?

He lifted the camera and snapped several frames, hoping to catch her spellbound expression with the Garden in the background. She seemed so far away all of a sudden . . . and lost in a beautiful dream he longed to share. His throat tightened and a lump settled there that threatened to choke him.

"You're losing it," he muttered. "She's got you turning into a poet."

"What'd you say?"

"Nothing. Just . . . nothing."

Finished with Amelia, he walked over to shoot some photos of the park. The wall only came to his waist, but he forced himself to walk up to it and look out across the road to the land beyond. A fine sheen of sweat popped out on his forehead and above his lip. He pulled a folded handkerchief from his pocket and wiped it over his face, before cramming it back in his jacket with a disgusted sigh.

Amelia turned and leaned her arms on the wall, gazing at the formations as though she'd never seen them before. Jeremiah backed up and took a profile shot of her looking intently into the mountains and beyond. What was on her mind? he wondered and wished he could ask her.

"Come on over, Jeremiah. You can shoot some more in a minute." She smiled and reached out a hand to draw him near. "Just enjoy it. Breathe it in, smell the scents of the mountains. Feel the awesome power of it."

Jeremiah chuckled. "You're quite the sentimentalist."

"I like beautiful things. This is one of my inspirations. Can you imagine living in that ranch house down there at the turn of the century?" She pointed across the road to White House Ranch.

He thought of his microwave, washing machine, satellite dish, and Monday night football. "Nope. Can't say as I can."

He looked at the whitewashed house sitting among its outbuildings, then down at the parking lot. His throat tightened, and he automatically stepped back from the wall. Amelia caught his arm and urged him to her side.

"You were doing fine until you looked straight down. Relax and enjoy the view."

Her plan hit him on the forehead like a board. "You think you're going to get me over this phobia, don't you?" He wasn't sure whether to be angry or amused.

She nodded slowly. "I know it isn't my business, but I can't stand seeing anyone so distressed over something like this."

"So why aren't you a shrink?"

"I might be one day, if I decide to finish college. What's wrong with that?"

He'd offended her. "Not a thing. I didn't mean anything by it. You'd be good at it." He rubbed his elbow. "I'm just not sure I like anyone analyzing me."

She stiffened. "I was only trying to help. If you don't want to go on, I'll take you back to the hotel."

Jeremiah saw the genuine hurt on her face. A shaft of pain hit near his heart. He hadn't intended to hurt her feelings, and she *was* only trying to help. Amelia must care about him if she was willing to help fight his demons. Isn't that the sort of thing you did for people you cared about?

He caught her hand and pulled her to him. She stopped a breath away. Her chin was tilted at a stubborn angle.

"Well?" she snapped. "Do you want me to take you back?"

"I'd love to have you take me."

She gasped, and he laughed as his lips claimed hers in a quick kiss. He pulled back and saw only surrender in her expression. Slowly, he brought his lips to hers a second time. Jeremiah intended to taste and tease, to feel the texture of her soft skin.

A snicker startled them apart. Jeremiah looked to his right and found a small boy standing a few feet away, a hand pressed over his mouth to stifle his laughter. Jeremiah sent a fake grimace at the boy, fighting his own laughter and released her. The youngster scurried away calling for his mother. Jeremiah smiled and looked at Amelia.

"What's the next part of your devious little plan?"

She looked embarrassed, and he could only assume it was because she'd been caught in her scheme.

"Well?"

"The Will Rogers Monument is an interesting place to go. I love to look at the pictures and read some of his material."

"Why do I get the feeling this isn't as harmless as it sounds?"

She hesitated. "I'd rather just take you there and let you see it."

"Amelia . . ." His tone held a warning.

"Um, it's on a beautiful forested hill . . ."

"And?"

"In a tower."

His stomach tumbled down to his shoes and landed with a thunk. It didn't take a genius to figure out her plan. "A tower. How tall?"

She shrugged innocently. "Gosh, I don't know."

He glared at her.

"Honestly, I don't know for sure. Maybe a hundred feet . . . or two."

He felt the blood drain from his head and the dizziness try to claim him. *Damn.* He snapped his shoulders back and locked his knees. Damned if he'd hit the concrete in a puddle of fear in front of Amelia, God and everybody.

"You've gotten it into your head I need desensitization, right?"

She had the good manners to look embarrassed. "Yeah, 'fraid so."

Dread of a process he'd read about warred with the warm feeling. She was starting to care about him, just as he cared about her. He had to smile, had to give in. This assignment was getting better each day.

"Okay, let's do it then." He grabbed his camera bag in one hand and captured her hand in his other one.

Jeremiah headed for the truck pulling her along in his wake, before he could change his mind.

CHAPTER SIX

Jeremiah tipped his head back and let his gaze climb the stone structure to the top, one row of blocks at a time. When it reached the top, the dizziness hit him hard, right between the eyes, and spread. Convinced that fear was a futile waste of human energy, he fought to abolish the physical response hitting his body. A few deep breaths and envisioning himself on the ground floor of a one-story building did no good. His head still spun, his stomach flipping in his belly. All of his usual tricks failed him.

Disappointment crept over his soul. Jeremiah didn't like to let anyone down, least of all himself. He dropped his chin to his chest and stepped back from the base of the tower. The clouds that hung overhead spit a few flurries of snow at him in a final insult. He shivered from fear and cold.

With shallow, shaky breaths creating small bursts of vapor in the cooling air, Jeremiah turned toward Amelia. "Not a good plan. Let's go."

"Jeremiah, you can do this." Her tone was comforting. "We can stay inside, but if we go out, the balcony walls are really high. You couldn't fall if you wanted to."

Demon fear fought for a place in his mind. Jeremiah forced it aside. His heart thumped against ribs he was sure would crack from the impact. He looked back at the monument and wished for a warm fireplace, a cold beer, and oblivion.

"It's a damn building," he grumbled. "A damn tall building."

Amelia put her hand reassuringly on his arm. "I'll be with you. Are you going to let something like this mess up your career and limit your life?"

He pulled a cleansing breath deep into his lungs and let it out with a huff. "No. No, I'm not."

Then Jeremiah took her elbows in his hands and drew her close, looking deeply into her eyes. "Don't expect miracles. It's going to take more than one trip up there for me to get comfortable with heights. A whole lot more." A horse-sized tranquilizer would help for starters, he thought.

She brushed his cheek with her fingertips. "I know, but it's a beginning."

"I'm not sure I can go to the top. Towers aren't exactly my favorite places."

"We'll take our time and just go as far as you want."

He wanted to be flip and make a wisecrack about her comment, but the concern in her voice undid him. He pulled her to him and kissed her, long and deep, thankful they were alone. The kiss didn't help his heart rate or his sudden arousal. The front of his pants tightened uncomfortably in a flash of heat. Jeremiah set her away and looked into her huge eyes before letting his gaze slide to her lips. Lips that trembled with need.

"We'd better go while I can still move." His voice was hoarse, and he cleared his throat. Jeremiah grabbed her hand. "Come on, I'll race you."

They started up the inside steps at a good clip until they reached the first chamber. Breathless, Amelia pulled him into the room. "Take your time. We'll get to the top. Let's look at the pictures."

Jeremiah glanced around at the vintage photos and newspaper clips, nodding his agreement. "Will Rogers was a great writer. Funny but astute."

"What's your favorite quote?" she asked.

"Hmm." Jeremiah hesitated. "I think the one about Congress. You know, 'Every time Congress makes a joke it's a law and every time they make a law it's a joke.' Or something like that." He chuckled. "I never remember which way around it goes."

Amelia's laugh was deep and warm. "That's rich."

"Most young women don't go around reading Will Rogers. How is it you know his work?"

"Dad loved him. I'm not sure if he loved his comments as much as he liked to read the work of a fellow pilot." She wandered around the small room. "Hey, look at these."

Photos of Will Rogers and his family doing roping tricks covered one wall.

"Have you seen his ranch in California?" Jeremiah

asked. "It's a park now, but they still use it for recreation."

"No, have you?"

Jeremiah nodded. "It's a beautiful place. There are polo fields and stables. Inside the house is a small pen where he actually kept a calf to practice roping."

Amelia crinkled her nose. "You're kidding."

"It's true."

"I think I like my livestock in the fields."

"That would be my take on it." Jeremiah glanced around the room. "Well, who's procrastinating, you or me?"

A smile spread across her face. "Maybe we both are. Come over here and get a look at the view from the window. It's gorgeous up here."

Jeremiah moved to her side as fear clutched around his heart and squeezed. You can do this, he told himself. Ignoring the constriction in his chest, he peered out carefully, straight ahead but not down. The clouds that had settled on the mountain obscured the view, but an occasional break allowed a distant view of the plains all the way to Kansas. For a man from a city the size of Phoenix, it looked like a whole lot of nothing but open space once you got beyond the city limits. A man could be free out there on the open range—with no tall buildings. He liked that idea.

"You're right. It's great," he said.

"You ready for another level?"

"Why not?"

They trudged up another flight of stairs hand in

hand. A second room filled with pictures stopped their ascent.

"We're half way up. Let's go out on the balcony." She headed for a door, but Jeremiah grabbed her hand, and she jerked to a stop.

"Let's look from the window."

"The wall's high. Come on."

Jeremiah hesitated, a frown creasing his forehead.

"This is really hard for you, isn't it?"

"Getting over heights?" He deliberately misunderstood her question.

"No, admitting you're afraid of something. It's a guy thing."

Her teasing smile eased the tension building in Jeremiah. He sent her a quirky grin.

"And just what makes you so smart about guy things?"

"I have two brothers and a father. Look, everyone has at least one fear." She slid her hand down the front of his shirt before poking him in the chest with one finger. "There's nothing wrong with that. It just makes you human."

"Okay, wise one, what's yours?"

Amelia chuckled. "That's easy—snakes." She gave an exaggerated shudder. "You know how they tell you to freeze if you come on one while you're hiking?"

"Yes."

"Before my mind could get that message to my legs, my body would be in the next county."

Jeremiah laughed with her, then silence settled around them. He looked at the door that led outside.

Panic tried to drill its way into his body and heart, but he shoved it away.

"All right. Let's go." He grabbed her hand and dragged her out to the small overlook. They leaned on the wall, looking down on the Cheyenne Mountain Zoo. Having Amelia at his side somehow gave him the strength he needed to fight back. Jeremiah was able to turn away from the fear, to ignore its power by drawing on her strength and courage.

He turned to say something to her, but the sound died in his throat. Amelia watched him, a look of deep concentration on her face as though assessing how he was doing. Her concern for him was easy to read in eyes that threatened tears.

Jeremiah captured her upper arm and brought her close. "What's wrong?"

Amelia didn't answer; she simply stared into his eyes.

Damn caution to hell. Jeremiah drew her into a strong embrace, closing his arms around her slim body. Longing for Amelia stole what common sense he had left. If Chuck Finwick didn't think his favorite reporter's take on her was objective enough, he could write the story himself.

She leaned into him, pressing her body to his as his arms tightened around her. He felt the thrust of her breasts through her light windbreaker and slid his hands down her back to draw her hips against his thighs. For a moment he held her close, her head on his chest. He slipped one hand into her hair and let the scent of woman and rose petals drift to his nose. Jeremiah cupped her cheek and lifted her chin with his thumb.

His gaze locked with hers for one long yearning moment, then his lips were on her own. Their mouths mated and the kiss deepened, heating Jeremiah's blood. Amelia's hardened nipples teased him so that he had no choice but to slip one hand up her top to caress her breast. She sighed against his lips and his tongue plunged deeper, matching hers stroke for stroke. When he reached under the edge of her shirt and tugged, seeking access to flesh, she pulled back with a groan.

"We can't do this." She stepped out of his resisting hands and pulled down her jacket.

"Right. Too public—let's go home." He was only too ready to make her his in every respect.

She shook her head. "We can't do that."

"Why not, Amelia? We're adults. Two consenting ones. What's the problem if we find each other more than a little attractive?"

Amelia stepped as far away as the small space allowed as though trying to protect herself.

"It's too soon. I don't jump into bed with every stranger I find attractive."

"Stranger? I've shared more details about myself with you than I have anyone else . . . ever."

"I appreciate that, but we need to slow down. Things are happening too fast." She pulled in a huge breath. "I'd be in bed with you in a heartbeat—"

Jeremiah groaned. Her soft words made his groin tighten even more.

She ignored him and continued. "And I don't know if that's the right thing for me . . . for us."

Hope leapt in his heart. He reached out to pull her against him, but she sidestepped.

"I think we've had enough of that and heights for today. Come on, I'll drop you off and give you the lowdown on tomorrow's flight."

She had turned off all that emotion like a light switch. Jeremiah frowned at her back as she went inside and headed down the stairs. What made this woman tick? One minute she was hotter than an eager bride on her wedding night and the next second colder than dry ice. He'd never understand women. With a shake of his head, he followed her out of the monument and to her truck.

The sexual longing he was suffering made him wish again that he'd never been given this assignment. But then he saw her lovely face when she turned to open the vehicle, saw the strength in her straightened spine. And he thanked his lucky stars and Chuck Finwick for sending him to Colorado to meet one Amelia Edith Dedham.

In front of the hotel, Amelia pulled up to the curb but left the engine running, making it clear their day was at an end. She put the truck in park and turned to a silent Jeremiah. The clouds had darkened considerably and now light rain mixed with snow was falling. The weather matched her mood.

"How are we going to fly?" Jeremiah asked. "Looks to me like winter's setting in."

She shook her head. "This will blow over later today, and it will be dry and sixty degrees tomorrow. That's the way it goes here."

"Darn." He gave her a cockeyed grin.

The tension between them eased for a moment, then settled back like heavy fog.

Amelia broke the silence. "Thanks for going with me. I enjoyed it." She picked at the edge of the seat cover. "I'm sorry about all this, about, oh . . . never mind." She kept her gaze on the floor.

"Look at me."

His order was soft but not to be denied. She raised her eyes to his.

"Something serious is happening between us. You have to admit that, Amelia."

She scanned his tan face, his thick wavy hair. Yearning grew deep in her belly as her heart tripped in an erratic dance. "I agree, but I want to go carefully. I'm not into one night stands, and you have a life in Phoenix."

"There isn't anything we can't work out if we both want to. Lots of people manage to maintain long-distance relationships and careers."

Pain filtered through her, darkening the fleeting hope that perhaps they could build a future together. "What about what I do for a living? Could you stand to see your girlfriend fly every day? To compete and try new things?"

His voice was quiet. "When something is important enough, you work at it."

"It's also worth waiting for. Let's just see what happens. Take our time and see where it goes. Okay?"

She heard his soul-deep sigh, saw the disappointed frown that pulled the corner of his lips down. Jeremiah picked up her hand and squeezed it reassuringly, then pressed a kiss to her fingertips before gently laying her hand on the truck seat.

"If that's the way you want it, that's the way we'll play it. Time is something I can give you."

Relief washed over her. He wasn't going to walk away from her yet. She'd been afraid he'd tell her to kiss off and die. Amelia realized that was the last thing she wanted. This man piqued her interest and grabbed her heart. What he did to her body wasn't bad either, she thought, blushing a little.

"Five o'clock, Memorial Park. I'll call if this weather doesn't clear."

Jeremiah got out of the truck. "Thanks, Amelia. I appreciate your help with the heights thing. I'm going to beat it yet." He seemed to fumble for words. "I'll see you tomorrow," he said quickly and shut the door on her reply.

Amelia watched him walk away and into the hotel lobby. She enjoyed the way he moved, the way his jeans hugged muscular buttocks and thighs. Desire swept her, leaving her hot and eager for his touch. It was as if her body already knew his and knew exactly how his hands would feel on her flesh.

Her body ached for more, for the total release joining with Jeremiah would provide. Amelia shook her head and forced herself back to reality. The reality that would take him away from her and back to his world in Phoenix. He'd never accept her flying, of that she was sure.

Disappointment tugged at her heart. Amelia wanted to know him in every way, before he left. Why had she said no to something she wanted so badly? What could it hurt to have a fling with such an intelligent, good-looking guy?

It could hurt plenty, her subconscious argued. She'd fall in love, the assignment would be over, and he'd be gone.

"Oh, shut up," she muttered. "He's gorgeous, funny and smart. And he has me talking to myself."

With a disgusted sigh, she put the truck in gear and pulled out of the drive, hitting the gas harder than she intended. The tires squealed and loose gravel and dirt created a billowing cloud in her mirror. Amelia eased off the accelerator and glanced around, hoping no one had seen the company truck peeling out of the parking lot.

Jeremiah Beach was quickly becoming bad for her. Bad for business and bad for her heart.

CHAPTER SEVEN

Amelia glanced at the sky and thought she had never seen one quite this light-drenched anywhere but Colorado. The balloon drifted free and rose into the turquoise expanse. She looked over the side to be sure they were clear. The launch site fell away, a grassy patch on which the crew scurried like eager children to put the equipment in the chase vehicle and follow her. Finished, they jumped into the truck and pulled out.

Amelia was hit by the same feeling of exhilaration that came with every launch. To be in the air, floating on the currents above the earth was awesome, to her way of thinking. Man had managed to transcend the boundaries that kept him tethered below soaring birds. Now she could be with the hawks on their morning hunt, could see them soar on a breeze and then dive at their prey. Amelia never felt as much at home in nature as she did in the air.

She pulled fresh air into her lungs and slowly let it slide from her body. What a beautiful day, she thought. Amelia glanced at Jeremiah as she blasted the burner to lift them higher. In spite of the sensation of floating and going nowhere, air currents were carrying them northeast at a good clip, above the field where the other balloonists hurried to launch.

A look of intense concentration replaced the one of sheer terror that had been on Jeremiah's face during the first flight. In a white-knuckled grasp, his hand wrapped a cable holding the gondola to the balloon.

She didn't think he could ever be completely comfortable with heights, considering his past. Disappointment claimed her, whether for him or herself, she wasn't sure. What would it be like to spend your life with a mate who feared and hated your passion? Didn't a person need the full support of their lover to accomplish their goals and dreams? What if that were missing? Amelia wouldn't allow herself to find out.

A frown trembled at the corners of her mouth as her smile faded. She was falling for this guy. She knew it. Not a good plan, she decided. Jeremiah Beach would finish this assignment and head south to Phoenix as fast as his long legs would carry him. He'd never set foot in a balloon again. Getting involved with someone who wanted nothing to do with her first love, her reason for being, was impossible.

What happened between Amelia and Jeremiah had to stay purely physical. An emotional involvement just wouldn't work. She would make darn sure of that. A good physical relationship was all it could be. The thought of his hands on her flesh intruded on her reverie. Her heart skipped a beat. Would sex be enough? Amelia doubted it. Her parents had just celebrated their thirty-fifth anniversary, and very happily at that. The standard marriage—two point three kids, a van, a house, a backyard, the whole thing—that's what she wanted. Halfway wasn't good enough. Amelia wasn't going to settle for that.

Oh, there was nothing wrong with physical. Jeremiah Beach made sheer lust flicker deep within her and roar to life like grassfire on the plains. The memory of his touch, the taste of his mouth, the way his smile carved sexy dimples in his cheeks and radiated into happy lines around eyes that sparked with color, only made her want him all the more.

A smile covered her face as she lifted her fingertips to her lips. Physical was definitely okay, but love meant infinitely more. She wanted an emotional commitment, too. The smile faded, and she dropped her hand.

She glanced at Jeremiah's face. A grim frown creased his forehead and dragged the corners of his mouth toward earth. What was he thinking? He looked withdrawn, lost in thoughts he might not want to share with her.

"Jeremiah?" Nothing. "Hey." She nudged him with her tennis shoe. "You in there?" She sent him what she hoped was a reassuring smile.

"Yeah, I'm here." His voice oozed dread.

Amelia laughed. "I can see your body there, but

I'm not sure about the rest of you. Are you doing okay?"

He hesitated, then nodded. "Yes." He raised one eyebrow. "As a matter of fact, it's not too bad."

"Great. Maybe you're getting used to it."

"I wouldn't go that far, but at least I'm breathing on this trip." A smile played across his face, then quickly disappeared when the balloon jerked. "What's that?" He snapped the question out.

"Just a gust of wind. It won't do anything but bump us. Don't worry, enjoy."

"Easy for you to say." He glanced around the balloon, watching her hit the controls again to lift them higher still. "How far up are we going?"

"I thought we'd just do another check of the instruments and make it an easy flight." Amelia dodged his question, thinking numbers might spook her passenger just when he was getting somewhat comfortable.

"How far, Amelia?"

She hesitated, then shrugged. "Oh, about nine thousand feet, I guess. That will let me do what I need to. If we stay under ten thousand, I won't have to mess with oxygen until the actual flight."

She watched his expression shift as he reacted to her response. Compassion threatened to make her bring the balloon down for another ground-skimming ride. But that wouldn't help him, and it wouldn't get her goal of a new record met, either. She wanted this record for her grandmother, and nothing was going to stop her from getting it.

"Think about the equipment and the operation of the balloon. Forget the numbers. When you consider Colorado Springs is already at about six thousand, we're really not up far at all."

Jeremiah grunted, then focused on her and what she was doing.

"Hey, I know what would help," she blurted.

He looked at her, a questioning tilt to his head. "What? Don't start that desensitizing stuff again."

Amelia laughed. "I can't hang you out over the side. How could I desensitize you up here?"

"I don't know, but I don't trust you for a minute, lady." He said the words with a mock growl.

"What you need is to be in control."

"You mean flying?"

"Sure." She tucked her hair behind one ear.

"You're joking!" His voice cracked.

"No, I'm not."

"No offense, but you're nuts." Jeremiah hunched his shoulders up around his ears.

"Think about it. Doesn't it make you nervous to ride with someone you don't know driving a car?"

"Not really."

"Oh, come on, are you telling me you don't care who's driving if the road is bad, icy or something?"

"Well. . ." He clamped his jaw, and she watched his gaze slide over the controls and up to the balloon.

She jumped on his indecision. "It's easy. My dad taught me when I was a kid. You can do what a child can, can't you?"

"Cheap shot, Amelia," he grumbled.

"Step over here, close to me." She grabbed the sleeve of his jacket and pulled him toward her.

When he stepped up, his body brushed against hers. She decided she'd just made a tactical error. Amelia's pulse went up like a skyrocket. *Focus, girl.* She caught his hand and brought it up to rest on the control she relinquished. Her hand closed over his, and she compressed the lever to blast the burner. After a few times, she dropped her hand and let him handle it, not caring about height for the moment.

The balloon started to drop, so she showed Jeremiah how to use the altimeter to gauge when to use the burner. As he caught on to the timing to keep them going higher, his jaw softened and a slow smile spread across his face.

"This isn't bad." The dimples appeared when he looked at her. "Not bad at all."

Her heart skipped a beat then started up again at breakneck speed. *Darn those dimples.* She fought to think clearly. "Good. Just keep us at this altitude then. When you see us start to drop, give it another blast of heat."

The balloon dipped and Jeremiah hit the lever and held on.

"Whoa, not too much. Just a few seconds at a time."

Amelia laughed with him and raised her gaze only to have it meet and lock with his. The breath clutched in her lungs as she was hit with a wave of desire to hold him close. What would it be like to spend a snowy Colorado day making love to him in front of her fireplace?

She struggled to focus on those eyes. Brown eyes that sparkled with gold flecks as the smile that lifted his full lips spread to his eyes.

Jeremiah had to look away for a moment. But only a moment. This woman was becoming special, too special. A sweet sensation of just plain lust ran hot and fast in his veins. Visions of throwing her to the floor of the gondola and having his way with her invaded his concentration. How long would the balloon float if they made love? His desire grew and throbbed. Jeremiah glanced down to be sure his jacket hid the proof that he wanted Amelia much too much. Maybe they could test the theory, see how long they could ignore the burner. Maybe he'd die happy if they tried it, and he was in her arms when they collided with the planet.

Remembering the sensation of her lips on his, her soft, willing body beneath his own tantalized him. The peaks of her firm breasts would push against his chest as he braced above her on his elbows. He could almost feel the velvet closure of her most intimate parts around him as he slipped inside of her. His body trembled with the power of his need for Amelia.

"Hey, look out. We're dropping too fast."

He jerked his attention back to the burner, gripping the lever in a death clutch. Their descent slowed.

"Sorry. I was, uh, thinking about something else."

Amelia chuckled. "Me, too."

He watched as a delicate pink blush rose from

beneath the neckline of her coat and spread over her cheeks. Her pulse throbbed at the base of her throat, moving her flesh in a steady rhythm. It was obvious she had been thinking along the same lines. Interesting.

"Look, we really need to put this on hold until later," she said. "Much as I'd enjoy it," she added.

He nodded slowly. "I hate to agree, but you're right." He raised one shoulder and let it drop. "I'm—"

The balloon jerked as another gust hit it. Jeremiah forgot what he was going to say and squeezed the lever.

Nothing happened. No burst of flame. No noise. No heat.

"We're dead," he said calmly.

"No, we're not—"

"Yes, we are," he argued. "Fate will not be denied."

"Jeremiah, listen to me. It just flamed out. That's not a problem."

"Easy for you to say." He gave an undignified snort. "We're about to be the bug on the windshield."

"Stop saying that and let go of the control." She put the palm of her hand on his chest and pushed him aside. "Give me a second, and I'll re-light the pilot."

He turned to her, knowing his face reflected the pleading in his heart. He was too young to die.

"Honest. When it fires, I'll take us down," she said.

"Good. That's good." He licked his lips, nodded and stepped back to the side to clutch the basket.

His heart was thundering and his stomach had developed a life of its own. Impossible or not, he was sure it was doing back flips in his gut.

The pilot didn't light on her first try. Amelia flicked her lighter and tried again.

Jeremiah relived the terrible night of the school dance as clearly as he had in a thousand nightmares. His body hurtling toward earth, arms flailing uselessly for a handhold to stop his fall. Then the crash onto the car and the mind-numbing pain that followed before he'd slipped into unconsciousness. Nausea sent bile into his throat as a fine sheen of sweat broke out on his forehead. He ignored both and watched Amelia.

She tried a third time. Nothing. Jeremiah's blood drained from his head to pool in his toes. He swallowed the softball that lodged in his throat and tugged to loosen the collar of his jacket. One hand stayed clamped on the suspension cable. A muscle in his jaw twitched with suppressed emotion.

At last, the flame caught and Amelia slowed their descent. She looked into his face, appeared to assess his state of mind, and shook her head. "We're going to land. I think we've done enough for today."

Jeremiah couldn't agree more.

Amelia brought the balloon down as gently as she could and watched as Jeremiah vaulted from the gondola the minute it touched the ground. He strode away across the open field with his hands crammed into his pockets. Amelia's heart ached for him. He'd been doing so well and now this had to spook him again.

She called out to the crew to take care of things and hurried to catch up to his ground-covering steps. Amelia had to trot to close the distance between them.

"Hey."

He kept walking as though he hadn't heard.

"Jeremiah." She grabbed his sleeve and pulled him to a stop. When he swung around, she took a step back from the raw emotion she saw reflected on his face. She'd never seen the muscle jump in a man's jaw before and could only assume he had his teeth clamped together. If she hadn't known he had no reason to be angry, she would have sworn he was furious.

"What the hell is wrong?" she asked. "What are you so upset about?"

He glared at her and forced his hands further into his pockets. She had the distinct impression he was trying not to grab her. When he remained silent, she tried again.

"What's wrong, Jeremiah? We're all right," she added in a soft voice.

"By the grace of God."

At least he was talking.

"A flameout is nothing. I know it—uh, surprised you. Are you angry with yourself for being bothered by it, or me for letting it happen? Neither one of us could help it."

"You don't get it, do you? It's not about me." He shuddered. "You. . ." His voice faltered, and he tried again. "You could end up dead in that thing."

"Is that what this is about? Darn it, Jeremiah, a person can end up dead in any sport—fall off a horse, ski into a tree, smack her head on a diving board—"

"None of those have quite the same effect as hitting the ground from ten thousand feet with no chute."

"Do you want stats? The numbers of safe flights compared to accidents?"

"No! I don't." His voice dropped to just above a whisper. "I want you to quit."

Amelia's heart dropped like a deflated balloon. "You . . . want me to quit flying?"

"That's right." He jerked his hands free and grabbed her arms, pulling her up nose to nose with him. "I don't want to read about you splattered on the ground somewhere."

Temper flared and raced through her body, heating her blood to a dangerous level. "And you"—she poked his chest with her finger for emphasis—"you think you have a right to tell me what to do because. . . ?" She hissed the last word.

"Because I care about you." He dropped his hands to run his fingers through his hair. A sorrowful sigh escaped from between his lips. "I don't want to see you hurt."

"What I do is no business of yours. I grew up flying and I'm not going to stop until I'm too old and feeble to manage it. Then I'll have my grandkids take me up."

Jeremiah frowned. "You can't mean to keep this up after you get married and have children."

"Of course I do. I intend to teach my kids to fly just like my dad taught me."

"What if the man you marry doesn't want you to?"

A heavy silence pushed between them like a wedge. Moisture filled her eyes. Amelia choked back her tears and raised her chin defiantly.

"I won't marry a man who isn't a flyer like me or at least one who doesn't respect my freedom to do what I love. My man will be someone who lives for the sky, or at least understands what having a passion is like."

Jeremiah's eyes narrowed and turned deep brown. The gold flecks in his eyes were no longer happy, but sparked dangerously. His dimples were gone, a deep frown in their place.

"Well, that lets me know where I stand," he said.

Amelia slowly unzipped her jacket and pushed it back to place her fists on her hips. "I'm sorry, Jeremiah, but you have no say in what I do." She lifted her chin a notch. "No one ever will. You write because you have to. I fly because without it my soul would crash and burn."

He stepped back and gazed into her eyes as though searching soul-deep for the truth in her words. Amelia dropped her gaze to the ground.

"Come on. I'll take you back to your car."

"Right. I want this story done, then I'll be out of your hair, for good."

Amelia dropped her hands from her hips. "That's probably best for both of us."

She headed to the truck barely able to see through the tears that filled her eyes, then overflowed to run unchecked down her cheeks. No one said a word as she slid behind the wheel and slammed the door. No one dared.

CHAPTER EIGHT

"Carrie, damn it, he's out of my balloon." Amelia paced as far as the phone cord in her office would allow. "He's caused nothing but trouble since he got here." She twisted the cord around her fingers.

"Now, it can't be that bad, dear," the older woman coaxed. "Give him another chance."

"Don't 'dear' me." Amelia slapped her open palm against her thigh. "He's a pain in the . . . butt, and he's grounded."

She stopped walking and rubbed at the throbbing behind her temples. Amelia slipped her hand around to massage the cords of muscle on the back of her neck.

A long pause vibrated over the wire. "What did he do to you, Amelia?"

He ripped my heart out. "Nothing. At least not yet."

"Well, in that case . . . I could call Lindsey—"

Not in a mood for games, Amelia cut her sponsor off. "Don't pull her out of your bag of tricks. Your friend Chuck sent a man who's afraid of heights to cover this flight. Beach is trouble, I tell you." The dead silence on the line got her attention. "Look, I'm sorry. He has me so upset I can't think straight. Looks like winter is going to come early, and I want this record before then."

"I know how important this is to you, Amelia, but advertising is the only reason I'm in it. We're spending a lot of money promoting your flight and my company."

Amelia sighed. The threat hovered between them. The breath whispered from her body in defeat. "All right. I'll see what I can do about him."

"That's the spirit. Let me know when you plan to go for it, dear, and I'll be there with bells on. I'll be sure the press is, too."

Amelia groaned. The woman knew every cliché in the book. "Right. I need two more days to fly before we go for it. If the weather's okay, I'll go for the record Saturday." She hung up the phone and turned to flop into her desk chair.

The sooner this was over, the sooner she could send Jeremiah Beach packing. A constriction closed around her throat, making it nearly impossible to breathe. Tears welled in her eyes and her hands shook. How had he made such an impact on her in a handful of days? She wanted him to go. She wanted him to stay. Neither way would make her happy, because either Jeremiah had to be present and unhappy or she had to get over losing him. Amelia faced a losing battle either way, and she knew it.

She dried her eyes and pushed her hair behind

her ears. Amelia straightened her shoulders and made her decision. At least one of them should be happy. She had to send Jeremiah away. No doubt he'd be taking her heart with him.

The next morning dawned clear and perfect for ballooning. Amelia raced from the house and joined her crew to head for the launch site. If she worked it right, she'd be in the air before he figured out where they were. She needed a day alone to figure out what was happening to her.

During the long, sleepless night she'd actually thought fleetingly of doing as he asked. Did she love him enough to give up something so special? Could she stop a thing as spiritual for her as flying? Amelia knew that would be impossible.

They parked and stretched out the balloon along a damp, grassy slope. Amelia slid downhill on the wet surface and slammed against the basket.

"Debbie, come on, get the fan running. Paul, move it, would you? I want this launch done in record time."

"Right, boss lady." Paul grinned at her. "Aren't you going to wait for Jeremiah?"

"No." Amelia moved to help spread out the fabric.

"Want one of us to go with you?"

He sounded hopeful, and Amelia hated to disappoint him. Crew members worked hard at the crack of dawn for small wages and the occasional ride.

"Sorry, I need to go alone. As soon as the record's

done, we'll all take a celebration flight, and I'll get someone else to drive for us."

Amelia glanced toward the road several times. At last, the balloon inflated, Amelia climbed in and fired the burner. A glorious sense of freedom washed over her as it always did with a launch.

As she floated into the sunrise, Amelia watched a dark green MG race into the parking lot. Ambivalence claimed her. She was glad he hadn't gotten there in time, wasn't she? She lifted her chin and threw back her slumped shoulders. Yes, this day was hers alone.

The car pulled into a space and slammed to a stop. Amelia saw Jeremiah jump out and look skyward, then jerk his baseball hat off and slap his hand with it. He threw it into the car and cupped his hands around his mouth. Whatever he yelled was lost to the distance between them.

Turning away, Amelia wiped a single tear from her cheek and focused on flying. Between blasts, the silence was profound. Nothing intruded on her space and a weighty peace settled on her mind. She caught the current and moved south toward the mountains. Her favorite ride was along the Garden of the Gods and in front of Pike's Peak. Amelia figured it was as close to God as she'd ever be.

Jeremiah Beach wanted her to quit. Amelia didn't think she could; she had to keep flying. But at what expense—losing Jeremiah?

As she listened to the silence, she knew the truth. She could never give this up. She'd quit breathing first. What was she going to do?

Jeremiah's image floated in front of her. She wished she could forget his smiling face, high cheekbones topping the deepest dimples she'd ever seen. She recalled all too well the warmth of his skin beneath her hands, the ridges of muscle that covered his chest. The remembered scent of male soap and musk tantalized her and stirred a very feminine desire for him.

Longing landed on her like ballast, threatening to drag her down. Her palms were damp, her pulse throbbing. Amelia wanted to fly to a mountain meadow and make slow, passionate love with him in a field of wild flowers. Her body was moist and hot, ready to receive him as her mate.

She gave an undignified snort. What on earth was wrong with her? Wanton lovemaking wasn't her style, so why was she suddenly yearning to spend the rest of her life doing just that with Jeremiah Beach?

The answer hit her in the middle of her chest and took the breath from her body. Jeremiah had stolen her heart. She was in love for the first time in her life. And, she feared, perhaps for the last time.

Jeremiah watched the balloon drift south. His heart went with it in the hands of the woman inside. The sound of slamming doors jerked him back to the moment.

"Hey, wait for me!"

He ran to the four-door truck and jumped into the back seat. Debbie and Paul looked at each other, then shrugged and Debbie pulled out of the parking area.

They followed Amelia in silence for an hour and a half. The unending silence wore on Jeremiah's nerves, and he fidgeted in the confines of his seat belt.

"Shouldn't she be calling in or something?" he asked.

Paul looked at his watch. "Soon."

The tense reply didn't make Jeremiah any less tense. "When is she coming—"

Scratchy sounds came from the dash-mounted radio. Jeremiah leaned forward to catch every word.

"Chase One, this is the Edith. Where are you?"

"We're heading south on one fifteen. We have you in sight."

"Stay with me. I'm looking for a landing zone."

The crackling died. Jeremiah never took his eyes off the balloon. Watching her up there was worse than being in the air himself. Sweat gathered on his face, and he wiped it away with the sleeve of his jacket. His fingers were twined together and clutched in a death grip.

Trees and bushes along the roadside whispered in the rising breeze. Wasn't that a problem? Jeremiah wondered. Didn't that mean a rough landing? He was helpless here if she had any trouble. Seeing her crash to earth like a bird shot out of the sky would be his only option.

"Like I could do anything if I was up there," he grumbled under his breath, berating himself for not knowing more about balloons. "You guys ever see her crash? Does that happen often?"

They looked over the seat at him, but simply shrugged, not commenting on his question.

"Look, Paul, give me a break, man. I'm really worried about her."

Paul turned in his seat.

"Paul," Debbie snapped. "She won't like you talking about her when she's not here."

"Why? Has she crashed before?" Jeremiah had to know.

"Crashes with balloons are really rare," Paul told him.

"But?" Jeremiah asked.

"She crashed once," Paul said—and then Debbie punched him one-handed in the gut. Paul sucked air into his lungs through clenched teeth and gave her a dirty look. "He deserves to know."

"Why would that be?" she asked.

"Because he cares about her. Any fool can see that."

Any fool but me, Jeremiah thought. "Tell me what happened." It was said quietly but was an order nonetheless.

"She was in the balloon with her grandmother the day she tried for the altitude record."

"And?"

Debbie cut them off. "This isn't his business. Look it up in the papers if you're intrested," she said to Jeremiah, glaring at him in the rearview mirror.

"Butt out, Deb. This is between them."

"Then keep your mouth shut and stay out of it."

Jeremiah watched the sparks fly between Amelia's crew members. Something was going on there, he thought. But his concern was Amelia, here and now.

"Come on, Paul. Spill it."

"The weather went bad. Thunderstorms built over the mountains and the wind came up. They aborted the flight, but couldn't get down quick enough to avoid the storm. It brought them down too fast and slammed them into the ground."

"My God." Dread filled Jeremiah. He knew what was coming as surely as if he'd been there.

"They crashed and her grandmother was thrown out of the basket. She hit her head against a rock outcropping and died at the scene." Paul grew quiet. "That's why Amelia insists on helmets in the balloons."

"And Amelia? Was she hurt?"

"Not too badly. She broke her ankle and wrist," Paul said. "We got her away from the scene as fast as we could, but she refused to leave until her grandmother had been taken care of. It was pretty rough."

"So you two have been with her a long time?"

"That's right," Debbie answered. "And we won't let anyone hurt her."

"Why isn't she terrified of flying?"

Paul shrugged. "Beats me. She was back in the air as soon as she got out of the hospital, casts and all."

Jeremiah's pride in her fought with common sense. "I suppose it's like falling off a horse. You have to get back on, sooner rather than later," Jeremiah said.

"Amelia said she wanted to do this for her grandmother." Debbie sounded reluctant to speak of it. "She said she felt close to her up there. It took her three years to get over it. Then she decided she had to do this flight for Edith."

"This blue balloon with the bomber logo belonged to Edith, didn't it? They crashed in it."

"That's right," Paul said. "Amelia wanted everything to be the same as before."

"With one exception." Jeremiah shook his head in wonder. If anyone should be afraid of heights, it should be Amelia. "She flies in spite of all that," he murmured. He was in awe of her amazing courage.

What kind of woman had he fallen for? One with guts and determination. One destined to fly. How could he ask her to give that up? The answer was simple. He couldn't. The question became, could he live with her flying? With her pushing the limits? Jeremiah didn't think so.

The balloon drifted toward an open field. Jeremiah glanced at the trees and bushes at the side of the road. They didn't move. Thank God the wind had settled; the landing should be gentle. His heart beat faster anyway as he watched her skillfully pilot the balloon to a soft set down. He had the feeling she could put it down on a postage stamp if she wanted to.

He took off at a jog and reached the gondola before Amelia climbed over the side. His only thought was to touch her, to hold her against him.

She yelped as his arms circled her from behind and dragged her out. Her feet barely touched the ground before she swung on him.

She flattened her hand on his chest and shoved. Jeremiah stepped back. He raised his hands in surrender when he saw her clenched fists.

"What on earth are you doing?" she demanded.

"Why didn't you tell me you'd crashed in one of these things?" The fear washed over him, but this time it was for her, not himself.

"You didn't ask." She turned to leave, but he grabbed her sleeve and pulled her back.

Jeremiah caught her upper arms and lifted her to her toes. Their faces an inch apart, he said, "I assumed if you'd been in an accident in a balloon you'd be dead."

"Put me down." She emphasized each word, leaving him no choice but to comply. Amelia drew a deep breath into her lungs. "Who told you about it?"

Jeremiah's gaze slid to her crew.

"Oh, fine, I have traitors on board."

Debbie glared at Paul and punched his shoulder. "I told you to keep quiet."

"Give it a rest. Let's get this balloon packed," Paul said. He grabbed her hand and led her away.

"Don't blame them. I coerced it out of Paul. So tell me, how come there wasn't anything about the crash that killed your grandmother in the clip file Chuck gave me?"

"I don't know. It was all over the newspapers." Disgust at the invasion of their privacy rushed back as though it had happened yesterday. Amelia saw camera flashes at the funeral, microphones shoved in her parents' faces as well as her own. One reporter had asked how she felt about surviving a crash that killed someone else, someone dear to her. That question still haunted Amelia.

A puzzled frown slid over Jeremiah's face, then lifted. "I'll be . . . Chuck must have pulled the material—knowing how I felt about heights. He didn't want to scare me off." Jeremiah rubbed his elbow. "Friend or not, I'm going to have a serious talk with that SOB when I get home."

"Look, I didn't want to talk about the accident then, and I don't now."

Jeremiah looked at her face and saw only resolute determination. "You won't give it up, will you?"

"I can't." Amelia shook her head. "It's a part of me. If I gave up doing something I love so much—well, I couldn't."

Acceptance settled heavy on his shoulder. "All right. I'll cover this story. Then I'm going back to Phoenix and forget I ever got into one of these damn things."

Jeremiah spun on his heel and walked away, leaving Amelia staring after him. A sense of loss settled over him. He wished desperately that he could change how he felt about heights and flying. That wasn't going to happen. He'd need a time machine for that—to go back and remove the fall from his past.

At the truck, Jeremiah turned to watch Amelia help Debbie and Paul wrap up the balloon. Her back was straight; her attention focused on the job. It was impossible to tell she had just been told someone she cared about would soon be leaving her behind. That he would never see her again.

Maybe she didn't care about him, maybe that's why she wasn't willing to give up the flying. A new kind of terror took his breath away. He might be kidding himself about how she felt about him, but that didn't change the fact that he wanted to spend his life with her.

The pain in his chest came close to what he'd felt hitting a car from the top of a tower. He lifted one hand and rubbed at the spot wishing it away. It didn't work. Like the other pain, this was going to take time to fade.

Amelia had become a part of his heart and soul. Jeremiah wanted her out of there, but how?

CHAPTER NINE

The thrill of an impending record flight was beginning to work its magic on Amelia. The fact that this one was special added a nervous tension to her mood. Her foot tapping to the blaring of a Chubby Checker tune on her favorite oldies station, Amelia vibrated with excitement. Tomorrow was the day. If everything worked right this last time, tomorrow would be a go. She'd already checked ahead several days—the weather was supposed to be perfect.

Amelia pulled into the park just before dawn with Debbie and Paul as dozing passengers. She smiled at them, knowing their excitement would build when the balloon came out of the trailer on the actual launch day and not before.

She spotted Jeremiah immediately. He stood a head above a group of men and women easily recognizable as reporters by their cameras and recorders. An emerald green jacket was fastened around his throat against the morning chill. She didn't have to see his eyes to know the color would bring them out, intensifying the gold flecks like sparks of fire. The jacket did little to hide his broad shoulders or the way his torso tapered down to slim hips and firm thighs. A blush kissed her cheeks as she chose a spot to park and unload.

Jeremiah glanced up and their eyes met briefly before a fellow reporter got his attention. A gentle smile warmed his face. Heat rushed through her veins as desire curled deep within her, as it did every time she saw him. What was it about the man that made her melt so easily, anyway?

A sudden realization hit Amelia hard enough to take her breath away. She was in love with a ground bird. How the hell had that happened? She slammed her fist against the steering wheel, forgetting she had an audience, albeit a sleepy one.

"You okay?" Debbie asked, straightening in her seat.

"Sure. Let's get this done."

Amelia's gaze slid around the circle of newspeople. Carrie had wasted no time in getting the word of their last practice out. Her sponsor was in this for the coverage, but no one seemed to grasp that Amelia did these flights for her own satisfaction. Publicity had never been her goal. She wanted privacy, but sponsors were a necessary evil.

"Come on, let's get to work." Followed closely by the others, Amelia jumped out of the truck and slammed the door.

Nearby, several other balloons were already spread out, waiting to inflate. Amelia knew from past experience that they were doing their own practice flights to get photographs of her balloon and flight.

Jeremiah strode across the lawn, followed closely by an entourage. "Morning, Amelia." His voice sounded strained. A quick look revealed a deep frown and tight lips. Why the change? Was it nerves, anger? Amelia couldn't tell.

"Jeremiah." She kept working, doing her best to ignore the other reporters without being rude. Their incessant jabbering brought memories of another flight rushing in, a far from successful flight.

Questions flew at her, jumbling into one another until she was unable to make out anything. She held up her hands. "Whoa, whoa. I can't understand what you're saying."

A woman shoved a microphone under Amelia's chin. "Miss Dedham, are you going for the record today?"

"No." She tried to return to inflating the balloon, but another reporter blocked her way. Darn Carrie anyway. One of these days, she'd get a real job, and then she wouldn't need a sponsor.

"Okay, folks. Let me give you a brief rundown, and then I have to go. Today is a final check for an altitude record in a Class AX-Four balloon. Tomorrow I'll be attempting to reach at least thirteen thousand and fifty feet."

"Is that as high as anyone's gone?" someone else asked.

"Oh, no. Balloons in other size categories have gone much higher with specialized equipment."

"Why do it? What's the point if others have achieved greater altitudes?" a third chimed in.

Amelia sent a quick help-me look to Jeremiah. He gave her a thumbs up and one of his ready smiles.

"I suppose it's like a midget racer going for a speed record," she said. "Other larger cars have gone faster than it can, but what is important is the record for that size vehicle."

The vision of her grandmother laughing and joking with reporters on the day of her try for the record flitted across Amelia's mind. Her grandmother had been much better with the media than Amelia. Edith Dedham had used her adventures to further the quest for women's equality.

Amelia thought about how much she wanted to share about her grandmother with these strangers. Her grandmother had been far ahead of her time, and Amelia wanted people to know that. She cleared her throat, trying to ease the lump that settled there.

"I also have a personal reason. My grandmother, Edith Dedham, was the last woman to try to set a new record in this class balloon. She died in the attempt. The balloon behind me belonged to her. Tomorrow the record will be hers at last—through me." Her eyes filled with tears, which she impatiently forced away. "Excuse me, I have to go. If you have more questions, I'll be down in about an hour, and I'll speak with you then."

As she spoke, the balloon finished filling and lifted into the air. Amelia turned and climbed into the

CHAPTER TEN

Frigid air slapped Jeremiah in the face as he cruised along Highway 83. He'd left the MG's top down in an attempt to keep himself grounded and alert. It would be so easy to get distracted, just thinking about wanting Amelia. Her slim yet curvy form slipped into his mind. Determination was carved in her proud stature and wrapped around her like a shield. Why couldn't he find a woman who liked things on the ground? The usual woman stuff, he thought. Horses or knitting or shopping or something?

Jeremiah snorted and would have kicked himself if it were possible. Amelia was intelligent and courageous. If she didn't do the things she loved, she wouldn't be Amelia. A heavy sigh escaped his lips.

A future for them wasn't possible. He wanted to have, to hold . . . and to protect. That was the last thing in the world Amelia would appreciate. She would take care of herself no matter what. Could he be an equal partner? Jeremiah doubted it. How could he, when he didn't like flying?

Jeremiah caught himself in mid-thought. He didn't like flying? Really, he hated flying . . . didn't he?

He had to admit flying wasn't as bad as he'd thought it would be. Maybe that was because she was at his side. A sudden vision of her close to him, the imagined feel of her warm breath against his cheek as they whispered words of love, made his heart beat so strongly he could feel it against his ribs.

Damn. He loved Amelia. What on earth was he going to do about that? She needed someone who loved the same things she did, someone who could support her ambition and record-setting spirit. She'd never have him.

Jeremiah shook his head impatiently. He couldn't do it, couldn't watch her fly off with experimental equipment to do things that had never been tried. He'd be old and gray inside of a year. No, their relationship would end tomorrow. He'd stay at a distance this evening, ask his final questions, write his story and head south. That was all there was to it. Their relationship stopped here.

He turned into Amelia's drive and parked close to the back porch. As he climbed from the car, Amelia stepped outside, wearing a clinging Chinese-style electric blue dress slit up to her thigh. The porch light ignited the gold in her hair.

Jeremiah forgot the polite greeting he'd had in mind and suddenly his tongue seemed too large for his desert-dry mouth. "Evening, Amelia," he finally got out.

"Better put the top up." She looked skyward, giving

him a glorious profile of her long throat and classic features. "Might snow a little later." She turned and slipped back inside, leaving Jeremiah with a view of her bare back and swaying hips.

"Oh, man. This is gonna be a long night," he muttered to the wind. He lifted one hand to his chest as the blood in his veins surged in a heated rush and pooled in his loins. His body tightened and throbbed as he tried to force aside the need that pulsed in his body simply from the sight of her.

He wanted Amelia now, always. He couldn't have her. What the hell was he going to do?

Jeremiah lingered over putting the top up on his car. He drank in several deep pulls of fresh, cold air to slow the racing of his pulse. When the hammering in his chest quieted, he stepped into the kitchen, took one look at Amelia and all was lost.

She leaned over the sink, rinsing her hands, the tantalizing shape of her hips revealed in detail by her skintight dress. A length of leg was exposed by the side opening of her skirt, allowing Jeremiah's gaze to travel from slim ankle to curved hip.

What did she have on under there? Sweat soaked the palms of his hands. He couldn't see a thing but golden skin.

The devil must have designed that dress to drive men crazy. Maybe hell wasn't so bad.

Jeremiah was trying to regain control of his thoughts and body when she looked over her shoulder at him and picked up a towel. She dried her hands in slow motion, patting and then slowly rubbing each long, slim finger before neatly folding the towel and placing it on the counter.

"How are you? Did you get much done this afternoon?" she asked nonchalantly.

"Yes, yes, I did."

"Good." She nodded at the food. "I'm hungry. We're going with Chinese. Hope that's okay."

"Amelia." It was all he could force between his lips for several moments. "You look—devastating."

"Thank you. I hope you don't mind, I've got a fire going in the living room. We'll have appetizers in there."

She picked up a bottle of wine and two glasses, turning to give him another view of long leg. At that moment, Jeremiah figured he'd follow her anywhere, anywhere at all.

He picked up the tray of food and, his desire increasing with each step, followed her to the fireplace. A long, low table was laid with a cloth of Oriental design. Napkins and chopsticks were already laid out.

"Have a seat. You can take the sofa. I like to sit down here." She pulled a fluffy pillow from the couch and dropped it on the floor across the table from him, then sank gracefully onto it. She sat back on her heels, pulling the fabric taut across her body. It gave Jeremiah a detailed outline of her full breasts.

"Uh, don't you want to sit in a chair? That looks uncomfortable."

Her smile curved kissable lips and made her eyes

sparkle. "No, this is fine, really. Here, try these steamed *dim sum.* I made them myself."

She picked up a meat-filled dumpling with a pair of ivory chopsticks, blew on it gently to cool it, and dipped it in a brown sauce. Amelia leaned toward him and offered the morsel, one hand cupped under it to catch any drops before they could fall in his lap. As if he cared.

Jeremiah couldn't breathe, how did she expect him to swallow? He took her offering, anyway, and tasted—nothing. He was too busy imagining what her own sweet flavor would be to care what she was feeding him. It might have been rattlesnake for all he cared at that moment. He couldn't think of anything but getting her in a large bed and making wild, imaginative love to her all night long.

"Well?" she asked. "Do you want more?"

Jeremiah choked and sipped hastily from his wineglass. Tears gathered in his eyes as he gasped for breath.

Amelia leapt up and slapped him on the back. "Are you okay? Be careful." She sat on the couch and patted his back again. "Can you breathe now?" She leaned against him, her arm around his shoulders, her breast pressing against his upper arm.

Jeremiah jolted away. "Amelia, whatever game you are playing at—don't. It's dangerous."

She pulled her arm away and lifted her glass to sip. A few drops remained on the crystal rim, so she wiped them off with her fingertip and then licked the drops away from her skin.

Jeremiah watched, mesmerized.

"Game?" she asked, finally.

"Don't be coy, it doesn't suit you. This isn't a good idea."

She shrugged and rose. Carrying her glass, she walked to a switch and dimmed the lights, flicked on some soft love ballads, and then moved to stand beside the fireplace. What little had been left to his imagination by the dress was gone as the flames turned her into a transparent vision.

He groaned. "You don't know what you're doing."

"Yes, I do." She nearly whispered it. "I want you, Jeremiah. In every sense of the word." She lifted her arms, inviting him in.

"How do you expect me to resist? You're offering me what any man would be crazy to turn down."

She said nothing, simply moved her leg to allow the fabric to part. His gaze made another trip from ankle to thigh. Every male part of his being protested his self-control. His eyes lifted to her face, a face that reflected a raw hunger and desire that matched his own.

"Please," she said.

Jeremiah was lost. He stepped to her and pulled her into his arms. His fingers sank into her hair as he pulled her head back to assault her lips. She opened to him and their tongues stroked and tasted.

Amelia etched the memory of his taste and scent in her senses. They'd have this night. He loved her; she knew it. Just as she knew he would leave.

She pulled her head back and gazed into his eyes.

They had gone deep green from desire, but still the truth was there. He'd be gone tomorrow, but they had tonight.

Amelia sank her fingers into his hair and let his lips roam over her throat and down. His large hands spanned her waist, slipped upward across sensitive ribs to cup her breast. Jeremiah circled her taut nipple with his thumb. Her murmur of pure pleasure was swallowed by his lips returning to devour hers in a mindless kiss.

Together they sank to the floor, the flames of the fire crackling beside them. Legs entwined, they touched and explored. Jeremiah's touch traveled up her long, bare thigh to cup her bottom. He pulled her against him.

Amelia slid closer to feel the pulsing need of his body against her belly. She laid her leg across his hips and pulled against his, drawing him closer still.

Jeremiah caressed the bare skin of her back. He found the closures at the back of her mandarin collar and slipped the hooks open. His lips nudged the silk brocade aside and found the pulse beating in the hollow of her throat.

The fabric slid from her neck, and Amelia leaned back to let Jeremiah slide it down to her waist. He propped above her on an elbow and stared at the creamy flesh of her breasts. He lifted his fingertips toward her, then dropped his hand.

"You're beautiful," he whispered. "I never dreamed how really beautiful you are."

He leaned over her to capture one rosy nipple

between his lips, and she sank her fingers into his hair to hold him against her. Amelia arched her back and pressed against his suckling lips. Desire curled through her, rising toward a crescendo. She slipped her hand between their bodies and found Jeremiah's erection. When she rubbed her palm over him, he grabbed her hand and brought it to his lips. He kissed her fingertips, then teased her palm with the tip of his tongue before clasping her hand against his chest.

"Amelia. This isn't wise." He pulled in a deep breath. "I'm leaving tomorrow. We both know that."

"I know." She ran her fingertip across the strong line of his jaw, gazed deeply into his eyes and loved what she saw there. "But I want tonight. Give me tonight, Jeremiah."

The only sound in the room was the snapping of flames on logs and the soft sigh that came from her as she lifted her lips to his, daring him to take them again. Jeremiah captured her eager mouth, then trailed kisses and nips down her throat, across sensitive breasts, to whisper over her belly. Amelia cupped his face with her hands and pulled him back so their mouths met once again.

Eager to feel his body, flesh to flesh, Amelia tore at the buttons of his shirt, then helped him shed his clothes. She rose gracefully and stood in the firelight, her dress hanging about her waist. Amelia watched the heat of desire deepen the shade of green in Jeremiah's eyes. Her gaze locked on his, she smiled as she undid the hooks that kept the dress trapped around her hips, and slid it off. The electric blue silk pooled at her feet, revealing her nude body in all its glory.

Jeremiah let his gaze travel the length of her. He lifted one hand to grasp hers and pulled her down to his side. His feather-light touch caressed her body, over breasts and downward to the juncture of her thighs. When he slipped his hand between her heated flesh, Amelia pressed against it, clutching his body to her own as waves of passion flowed through her.

As his lips mated with hers, he slid into her. Her body moved in rhythm with his as she closed over him. Together they exploded in perfect unison, one body, one soul. A single tear slipped from the corner of her eye to slide across her cheek from the beauty of their joining.

They lay coupled together in the flickering light of the fire. Amelia wrapped her arms tighter around his body and stopped him when he would have moved aside.

"Stay—just like this, please. Just for a few minutes."

He gently did as she asked, loving her in his arms, wordlessly grateful to keep her so close. Finally, the logs burned low and the room began to chill.

"Amelia?"

"Hmm?" She snuggled closer to his side, sliding one hand into the hair on his chest to tease and twist the curls.

He grabbed her fingers as she felt his body twitch against her thigh. Amelia smiled in the dim light and teased his nipple with the tip of her tongue. His body responded to her, coming to life again.

She'd never had such power over anyone, especially a man like Jeremiah. The headiness of it was not lost on her.

Jeremiah laughed. "Stop that. You're incorrigible. He gave her behind a loving slap. "Do we plan on eating sometime tonight?"

Her smile faded. "You're all I need, Jeremiah. I could live on this." She rolled over to straddle him and kissed his throat. Jeremiah's pulse leapt, then pumped against her lips before she let her kisses travel down his body. His contented sigh was the last sound she heard for a long time.

They curled into each other like spoons, facing the newly rekindled fire. He slipped his hands around her body and let one hand rest on her breast. She scooted back against him until not even air got between them.

The tiny sound of a ringing phone infiltrated their peace. Amelia turned to look at him. "That yours?"

"Yep, the outside world invades. Let's ignore it." He made a face at her and took her arm to nibble from her wrist to her throat.

She laughed at his antics. When the ringing persisted, she nodded toward the sound. "Aren't you going to answer it?"

"If you insist." Jeremiah groaned and grabbed for his jacket. He pulled the cell phone from an inside pocket and flipped it open.

Amelia rose and slipped into her bedroom as he answered the call. Covered by a scarlet silk robe belted at her waist, she returned. Something in his tone kept her from clearing away their uneaten food and wineglasses. She leaned against the door frame, her arms wrapped around her rib cage under her breasts. Dread settled over her like an oppressive summer storm. She knew without him telling her that Jeremiah would be leaving soon, going back to his own life without her.

"Right. Okay, Chuck. Tomorrow's the final try—assuming everything goes well—and then I'm available."

She couldn't hear the other end of the conversation, only read the disturbing creases between Jeremiah's eyes and hear the seriousness of his voice. His entire demeanor had changed to one of a watchful predator.

"I'll take it. Make the flight arrangements. I'll be in Phoenix day after tomorrow—late."

He looked up at her and smiled. It was a weak attempt at reassurance, but Amelia saw straight through it. His gaze skittered away quickly, as though he didn't want to face her.

Jeremiah shut off the phone and reached for his pants, pulling them on before he turned to face her.

Unexplained fear gripped her. She knew he'd be leaving, but this was different. Something told her this wasn't just him going home.

"Where are they sending you?" she asked quietly, praying for a simple answer. Amelia wiped damp palms on her robe, then twisted her fingers together.

"Persian Gulf. Things are heating up again, and Chuck needs a war correspondent."

"War . . . my God. It is going to come to that?"

He shook his head. "Who knows? But Chuck needs someone in the region just in case, and he assigned it to me."

Amelia's fear was quickly replaced by anger. She straightened from the door frame and glared at him. "You . . ." She stopped and tried again. "You think what I do is dangerous. You can't stand to live with my flying, but you are voluntarily going to a war?" She whispered the last.

Jeremiah shrugged and crammed his hands into his pockets. "I guess you could look at it that way. I cover all kinds of stuff, not just human interest stories."

"Stuff," she snapped. "Like?" she prompted.

"Undercover crime, drug deals and things. Uh, guerrilla warfare in Africa. You know—stuff."

She stood in front of him and braced her hands on his chest. Amelia shoved, caught him by surprise and landed him on his backside on the couch.

"You son of a bitch." She pointed at him. "You never said a thing to me about these other stories. You only hinted at the other things you write." Amelia paced between him and the fireplace. "I'm the one doing all the dangerous stunts, you said, knowing perfectly well the work you do is far more dangerous than mine." She tucked her hair behind one ear. "I don't believe this."

His mouth had opened when he landed, and he slowly closed it and got to his feet.

"I guess the danger is relative. Kind of depends on what you're used to, Amelia." He reached for her, but she sidestepped him.

"You aren't willing to put up with my flying, but I'm supposed to watch the man I love go off to war-torn countries. Well, now we both know where we stand."

A great emptiness settled in her heart. Amelia knew it would be a long time before something filled its place.

"Look—"

She cut him off. "Good night, Jeremiah. Sorry we never got around to dinner. You can show yourself out." She spun and ran to her room before he could see the tears slipping down her cheeks. Inside her room, she leaned on the closed door as the tears dropped onto her scarlet robe. Her head dropped against the wood as she listened for his footsteps and then the quiet closing of the back door.

Jeremiah was gone. She'd face him tomorrow. For tonight, she'd simply try to forget and to heal.

basket, Jeremiah close behind her. She studied the grim lines around his eyes. Sorrow settled around her heart—the pain that comes when someone you care about doesn't understand your feelings, much less share them.

"You don't need to go up, Jeremiah. Surely you have everything you need for your story."

"I want to go up with you." The frown that formed belied the truth of his statement.

"Uh-huh, about as much as I would want to report on a drug cartel in Colombia." Amelia shook her head. "You've got your world, I've got mine. Stay here."

"I want to go on this practice flight with you, then we'll do the record."

"No. I'll do the record. You can't go." Yet she felt a heartbreaking sense of disappointment, which surprised her. She had always preferred to fly alone.

He turned to her before they could launch. "What the hell are you talking about? I'm supposed to cover this story from start to finish."

"And you will, from the ground."

"Like hell." He grabbed her arms and pulled her close just as her hand closed on the controls to take them away from the watching eyes of reporters and photographers.

Cameras flashed.

"Let me go." Amelia tugged uselessly at her arm and thought seriously of doing damage to Jeremiah's most prized body parts. "You're making a spectacle of us."

"I don't give a damn. I'm not staying down here waiting and watching the clock."

Amelia heard his voice catch, watched him struggle to speak.

"I'm not watching you float away from me, Amelia."

"Yes, you are." It was said softly but brooked no argument. She lifted her hand and touched warm fingertips to his cheek. "I'm sorry, really, but the rules for a women's record require the crew to be all female. Besides, I can't waste weight with a passenger or extra oxygen tanks."

She watched as he blanched.

"Oxygen?"

"Sure, going up over ten thousand requires tanks. You can really do without, but it's an FAA regulation. I told you about using it a couple of days ago."

"Guess I wasn't listening." Jeremiah let go of her and moved to the edge of the gondola to hang on. "I wanted to help you." He looked a tiny bit sullen, just enough to make her smile.

"You can, by keeping the other reporters under control and cheering me on from the ground." Amelia shook her head. "I'm not really sure why the media's even getting into this. It's not like I'm going around the world nonstop or something."

"Some of it is morbid curosity. Your grandmother died trying this. What's going to happen to you? Carrie's made the most of it in order to get more media coverage of her sponsorship."

"I suppose you're right. I just wish this could have been private. I'm not doing it for publicity."

"I know."

Amelia glanced over the side. "What on earth are those fools doing?"

Jeremiah dared a peek below them. A balloon sporting rainbow colors was coming up faster than he and Amelia were drifting away.

"They're going to ram us!" he yelled.

Her mind flashed over what she needed to do. "No, they're not."

Amelia hit the burner, long and hard, praying for a quick lift. She kept one hand on the controls and her other on the side of the basket to peer below. The other balloon pilot didn't stand a chance of seeing her directly above him. His envelope completely obscured his view.

The roar of the other balloon's burner filled the silence when she let off hers. Terror clutched at her heart as the memory of another rapid descent flashed into her mind. Her attention was diverted from flying for a split second. Was she going to crash in her grandmother's balloon again? This time she'd see Jeremiah slammed to the ground instead of her grandmother.

Jeremiah . . . she'd be damned if she'd let him hit the ground a second time. He'd never go up so much as a flight of stairs if that happened.

People on the ground shouted and waved their arms and jackets. Someone on the radio appeared to be trying to contact the pilot. Amelia guessed that he was looking skyward just as she usually did and wasn't seeing her balloon at all. Even if he did, it was too late to deflate fast enough to miss her.

Amelia knew shouting was useless. The pilot would never hear her. The only hope was to get higher and drift to the side before he came up under her. If there was a collision, she didn't know what might happen, even though he would undoubtedly get the worst end of the deal. Fear for Jeremiah claimed her and numbed her brain for an instant, then passed as quickly as it came. She had to concentrate.

"What's going to happen if he hits us?" Jeremiah looked at the ground. "How high are we—a couple hundred feet?"

Amelia ignored his questions. "Grab the bag tethered to the outside and open it."

Jeremiah remained frozen to the floor.

"Now!"

Jeremiah jumped and pulled the gym bag in. He knelt on the wicker floor to unzip it. The bag carried three helmets.

"Put one on," she ordered.

"Like that will help—"

"Do it!"

He slowly stood and handed one to her. The implication was clear. He would if she would. Amelia pulled hers on and fastened it between blasts of heat.

She peered over the side again. "Son of a bitch. He's gaining on us. Hang on!"

The other balloon hit them from below but slightly off center. Their gondola shimmied and shook as the balloon fabric mushroomed around it before falling away. Amelia watched a foot-long tear open in its deflation vent, and heated air hissed through the gap as the balloon began a rapid descent.

Jeremiah watched, his eyes wide. "Are they going to crash?"

"Not if that pilot's any good. If he keeps heating the air to replace what they're losing, he should slow down and just have a bit of a rough landing."

Amelia jerked off the helmet, thankful she wouldn't need it. Jeremiah followed her example, heaving an audible sigh of relief. He raked shaking hands through his hair before moving to stand at her side. Together they watched the balloon drop to earth, hitting and spilling out its passengers as the gondola tipped over.

People on the ground ran to help. Others were furiously shooting pictures of the scene.

"Do you think they're okay?"

"Looks like it." Amelia smiled, trying to reassure him. "I need to land and check on things. You got off easy today. This is a short flight."

"Right. We had a mid-air collision and I got off easy. That guy scared me half to death."

"Oh, you're fine." Amelia fought to sound cheerful. "At least today is your last flight. You don't ever have to go up again."

She watched as he frowned and became lost in thought.

"Aren't you glad?" she asked. A flicker of hope sprang up in her heart.

"Sure," he answered gruffly. "Yes, that will suit me just fine."

Jeremiah ran the back of his fingers across her cheek and locked his gaze on her own. Fire raced over her skin at his touch, and Amelia bit her lower lip to keep it from trembling. She wanted to slide her hands inside his shirt, to find heated flesh. And more. She needed to feel him against her, naked body to naked body.

"I'll miss you, Amelia." He looked up at the gigantic beautiful balloon keeping them airborne. "I can't honestly say I'll miss this, but it has been an . . . enlightening experience."

She tried to speak but her throat was dry, and she had to swallow. "It's best this way. Tomorrow you can write up this story and head home." Her heart ripped in half, she was sure of it. "We'll talk later."

She landed in the open, setting the gondola down gently. The media mob headed straight for her as she stepped over the wicker side. The microphones were back and the cameras were flashing.

"Ms. Dedham, are you hurt?"

"Is your balloon all right for tomorrow?"

"Are you going up again today?"

Jeremiah stepped between Amelia and the reporters. "Yes, she's fine. Yes, it is, and no, she's not. Ms. Dedham will speak to you all again tomorrow morning."

Grateful for the interference, Amelia ignored her slight irritation at Jeremiah taking over.

He tugged on her hand. "I want to talk to you."

They turned and moved away from the disgruntled reporters as Debbie and Paul packed the balloon. Under a huge pine, Jeremiah stopped walking.

"I need to get a final angle on this. Can I come by later today and see what you do the night before? How you feel and all that?" Jeremiah shrugged. "Then after the flight, I'll finish with what it's like to set a new record and that will be that."

"You're assuming I'll succeed." A soft smile crossed her face. "I might not, you know."

"You will. I've never seen such a determined woman in my life."

"How do you feel about that? Do you like strong women?" Hope never seemed to die, she thought ruefully.

"Can't say I ever thought about it, but I like you, so I must. I think it's a new experience."

She looked at his face, saw a spark of something. . . desire, love, she wasn't sure. If he loved her enough, wouldn't he work at getting into the flying?

You have one last chance, you idiot, she told herself silently. Go after what you want!

Jeremiah seemed to sense her indecision. He stepped close, too close. Her heart thundered away. Desire heated and flared, and her body ached with need.

He's leaving, a little voice seemed to whisper.

"I don't care."

"What?" Jeremiah raised a quizzical brow.

"Nothing. Just arguing with myself." Seeing him alone wasn't a good plan.

He's leaving and going to break your heart, the voice whispered again.

"He may as well do it right and take my body, too," she murmured to the wind. "At least I'll have memories."

Jeremiah cocked his head to the side, a lock of hair falling across one raised brow. "You all right, Amelia?"

"Yes, yes, I am." She took in a deep breath and blurted out, "How about dinner?"

Jeremiah hesitated. "Are you sure that's a good idea? We can talk in your office."

"Of course it's a good idea," she said with more conviction than she felt. "You're coming over to get the story, and you have to eat dinner, right?"

"Sure."

"Then do it with me."

A smile spread across Jeremiah's face, and he winked at her. "I'd love doing it with you, Amelia."

Amelia struggled to keep her balance, bracing her hands on his chest to steady himself. She leaned into him, raising her lips slowly toward his. Jeremiah slipped his hands up her arms and pulled her against his hard body. Their lips joined and fire flashed. Amelia's lips opened to his as she planned to open her body and soul to him. The kiss deepened. . . until she remembered that they had company.

Amelia wished with all her being that a pack of scandal-hungry reporters were not standing at the truck, watching them.

She wanted to drag Jeremiah to some hidden place

CHAPTER ELEVEN

Jeremiah watched Amelia fend off the reporter's questions. Dressed in jeans and a sky blue jacket, she looked like a teenager, not an experienced pilot. His gaze slid over slim hips and legs to her tennis shoes. Desire hit him hard. Just the sight of her was enough to make his hormones rage and his body take control of his brain. Whenever he got close to her, chaos reigned.

She appeared cool and calm, a long way from what he was feeling. An older man and woman stood on either side of her. He guessed they were her parents. They seemed to be providing moral support in the face of flashing cameras and microphones. Jeremiah noted that she looked a great deal like her father, but with her mother's coloring.

His gaze slid back to Amelia's face. She showed no visible signs of what had happened between them the night before, much less any trace of sorrow over his impending departure. Jeremiah clamped his jaw, its muscle twitching. Maybe she didn't give a damn.

Then his gaze met hers as she scanned the crowd. And he knew. The pain was clear to see if you knew her well. Amelia was a good actress; he'd give her that. The realization that he had hurt her didn't make him feel better. Regret was quickly added to the growing list of emotions that besieged him. Evidently Amelia had the power to turn him into a quivering mass of feelings. The sooner he left the better.

He saw a microphone pushed under her chin, which jerked him to the present.

"Any predictions for today's flight, Ms. Dedham?" the reporter wanted to know.

Her laugh was easy. "Of course, I'm going to set a new altitude record for my grandmother."

"What about the weather?" another asked. "Isn't a cold front coming through?"

She nodded, infuriating Jermiah when she carelessly tucked loose hair behind her ear as though she hadn't a care in the world. "That's true. But it won't move in until late today. I'll have plenty of time to reach the height I want and get down before the clouds build."

Jeremiah glanced skyward. Thin white veils already filtered across the mountains. Billowing clouds oozed around the sides of Pike's Peak and between the lower peaks. The cold front was rolling in fast, despite her assurances.

"Ms. Dedham." Jeremiah drew her attention and the other reporters fell silent. "What about those clouds?" He nodded toward the mountains, as unseen fingers grabbed his gut and twisted. The storm was building faster than she'd admit, he was sure of it.

Amelia looked into his eyes, seemed to delve into his soul, seeking answers of her own. She pulled back and answered, "not a problem. They won't develop into anything until later. If you'll excuse me, my crew has the balloon ready and I need to get going. Thanks for coming out."

"Wouldn't it be prudent to wait?" he persisted.

"No."

"Perhaps you have something to prove?" He heard a gasp from the older woman he knew was her sponsor, but kept his attention locked on Amelia.

"No, I never try to prove anything to anyone but myself, Mr. Beach."

Cameras flashed their direction and Jeremiah scowled.

"Is there a personal relationship to add to your story, Ms. Dedham?" a female reporter asked.

"No. My personal life is off limits." She pulled Carrie close as her parents stepped aside and turned to the other reporters. "This is my sponsor. She can answer more questions about the flight while I'm gone."

Amelia turned and strode toward the balloon as it rose above the basket. Jeremiah matched her stride for stride. He caught her elbow, and she came unwillingly to a stop.

"I don't have time for this, Jeremiah. I have to go."

"I don't like the look of the sky—"

She cut him off with a jab of one long finger into his chest. "*You* don't have a thing to say about this, remember? I do what I want, when I want. You didn't want to be part of my life, so butt out!"

Amelia pulled away from him and headed for the gondola.

"Please, wait a day or two until this front moves through."

She kept walking, her hands crammed into her pockets.

"Damn it, Amelia. I don't want you to end up like your grandmother."

When she slowly turned to him, the pain he had caused her was all too evident. "That was a cheap shot."

"I'm sorry, but I'm afraid for you."

"You should only worry about things you can control, and you don't control me. I do. The weather will hold for a few hours, I'll be done, and you will be out of my life—forever."

Amelia spun on her heel and strode to the basket without looking back. He watched her go, knowing what she said was true. He would leave her before the end of the day. Pain bolted into his heart and stole his breath away. This should have been a simple assignment. How the hell had he let it go so wrong? Devastation lurked at the edge of his mind. What was he going to do without her?

The sound of a slamming truck door reverberated across the field as she launched. Jeremiah swung toward the sound and took off at a run.

"Debbie! I'm going, too."

The truck slid as she stomped on the brakes to avoid hitting him when he skidded into her path. Debbie rolled down the truck window and leaned out.

"She doesn't want you with us. You'll have to follow in a car if you want to. Besides, all female means all female."

Jeremiah pointed at a man tucked in the back seat. "Who's he?"

"An official observer."

Jeremiah glanced at the small man making notes on a clipboard. "I'm a reporter. Don't know a thing about crewing or balloons. Can I come along as an unofficial observer, member of the press and all that?"

The man shrugged. "Sure."

Debbie glared at Jeremiah, then jerked her head toward a rear door. "Hurry up."

Jeremiah jumped in and shut the door as she sped out of the parking lot. He saw Amelia's parents pull out right behind them. Three chase trucks and four news crews attached themselves to their vehicle, following so closely they appeared linked like the cars of a train. He understood their need for news, but wished they'd leave Amelia alone.

Amelia. He swung back to find her. Amelia's balloon was traveling fast; too fast, it seemed to him.

"Why is it going that quickly?"

"There are some strong winds up there, that's all. She's going to have a good ride today," Debbie said.

"What do you mean?" Fear clutched his lungs, forcing the breath from his body.

"She's headed north-northeast. Should be interesting."

"And that's a problem because?"

She nodded ahead of them, her line of sight following I-25 north to the mountains. "It's higher there. The cold front will hit Palmer Divide and Monument first . . . and the wind."

Crackling sounds from the radio interrupted.

"Debbie, you there?"

She pulled the mike from the dash and spoke into it. "We have you in sight. How's it going?"

"Great. It's beautiful up here. No problems, moving up as planned. Stay with me."

"Right."

Stay with her, he thought. I'll stay with her long enough to wring her neck for scaring me half to death.

Jeremiah turned to the official. "Aren't there rules about not going up in bad weather or something? Why didn't you make her delay the flight?"

"It's up to her to decide when she wants to make a try for the record. We only observe, we don't offer opinions to the pilots."

"Swell."

They followed the highway for thirty minutes, then Debbie swerved off at an exit.

Jeremiah jerked his gaze from Amelia's balloon to Debbie. "What are you doing?"

"She's changed direction."

"I can't see any difference."

"Well, I can. I've been chasing her for three—"

The rasping sound of the radio grated on Jeremiah's already raw nerves and cut Debbie off in mid-sentence. Things began to happen fast.

"Debbie?"

"Yes."

"Where are you? I'm getting jerked around some in the currents. I've . . . shifted . . . "

"Amelia, we're losing you. How high are you? Are you ready to come down?"

"I've hit . . . thousand . . . almost there."

"Repeat, Amelia. We couldn't read you."

"Twelve thousand. Almost there."

Jeremiah's mouth and throat dried. Swallowing was impossible. Nothing would have gotten past the lump in his throat anyway, he was sure of it. She was going to achieve her dream. Pride warred with fear. When she landed, he'd tell her how proud he was, then he'd kill her.

"Thirteen, fifty. We did it!" Amelia shouted into the radio.

Jeremiah grabbed the radio from Debbie. "Come down! That's good enough."

"Going higher. Want to add to the record."

"Get down here," he shouted.

"Stick with me, Debbie. Moving northeast now."

"Alice, get that, will you?" Debbie nodded at the mike Jeremiah still clutched in white fingers.

Paul's replacement for the day pried the mike out of Jeremiah's hand.

"We read, Amelia." Alice scanned the county map in her lap and pointed to a road leading northeast between the trees. "Go that way."

'We're going to lose her if we go in there." Jeremiah looked skyward and saw nothing but tall pine trees. "Where's she going to land?"

"It opens up again in a few miles. She'll find a spot."

The abrasive sound of static filled the heavy silence that bloomed in the truck.

"Fifteen thousand." Her voice was muffled.

"Why does she sound like that?" Jeremiah looked at the observer. "What's happening?"

The man's gaze slid across Jeremiah, and he shook his head. "You really should relax. She just has an oxygen mask on, that's all."

"Right, okay." Jeremiah's heart stopped, then hit his ribs in protest. He slumped against the seat, swearing vengeance on the woman he loved. He couldn't stand to be with her. He couldn't stand to be without her.

"Debbie, get ready. Coming down."

Relief washed over Jermiah.

"Catch up if you can. Ground wind gusting," Amelia added.

Relief drained away. "What's the deal?"

"She's probably going to have a wild ride coming down. The clouds are building and the breeze is picking up." Alice shrugged. "May drag the balloon until it deflates."

"Drag it where?" Jeremiah still saw only forest.

"There's a large clearing in another few miles. She'll probably shoot for that."

"Oh, God." Jeremiah wiped the sweat from his forehead with a shaking hand.

Debbie met his gaze in the rearview mirror and smiled at him. "Chill out, Jeremiah. She's done lots of landings in worse than this. She'll be fine."

"She may have, but I haven't." A smile tugged at the corners of his mouth. "I'll be glad when she's landed."

"There she comes!" Alice pointed to a wide spot in the road. "Pull it over. Let's go—she's coming down too fast!"

Jeremiah leapt from the truck and outdistanced the others quickly, running as fast as he could. He stumbled once on the rough ground, recovered and charged toward the balloon, calling out Amelia's name as he ran.

The basket slammed against the ground, throwing Amelia over the wicker edge. Jeremiah threw his body across the tipped-over basket, trying to slow it as the wind caught the balloon and dragged it toward the trees.

"Amelia!"

"Grab the . . ." she screamed. But the rest of her words were swallowed by the wind. The rush of his blood and his own pounding pulse were all he could hear clearly.

Jeremiah watched as Amelia rolled across the grass, jumped to her feet and dove for the basket. She missed, and he saw her disappear below the edge of the gondola. A gust caught the balloon and lifted it from the ground, pushing it skyward.

"Damn! Not alone . . . oh, God!" He looked over the side, trying to decipher the instructions being yelled at him by the ground crew.

Amelia watched in horror as the balloon launched itself. Jeremiah couldn't go up alone. She dove again and grabbed a rope handle hanging from the outside of the basket. Swinging against the wicker, Amelia screamed his name over and over. Sweat gathered on her hands, making them slick. She pulled herself up far enough to wrap the short rope once around her wrist, praying for the strength to hang on.

She glanced toward the ground that rapidly dropped away beneath her. Her parents and crew were yelling and waving wildly at Jeremiah. Finally, she saw his face peer over the side.

"Amelia!"

"Get me in, dammit. Reach over and pull me in before I fall."

His face was paste white, and she could see sweat rolling down his face. Every ounce of blood in his body seemed to have drained.

"Jeremiah, focus! Lean over here and grab my hand," she shouted. "Help me!"

She watched him fight to breathe, saw his jaw tighten, then he was reaching over, stretching toward her. Their hands missed by inches. Amelia knew she'd never survive a fall from this height. And Jeremiah wouldn't know how to get the balloon down in this wind. They'd both end up dead.

"Come on. You're going to have to get farther out," she called.

He shook his head. "Can't."

Amelia glanced toward the earth now far below. "Yes, you can," she said. "Hook one foot in the equipment harness and throw the other leg over the side so you can reach me."

Jeremiah looked around, then shook his head.

"Now! Before it's too late!"

She watched sheer terror race across his face, then resolve seemed to replace it. Amelia knew he was as terrified as she, if not more so.

Jeremiah popped his leg over the side and leaned down to grab her.

Amelia locked her gaze on his. "Don't look down, just look into my eyes," she ordered.

She latched onto him with her free hand, then unwound the rope to grab with her other one. His fingers locked around hers like a steel vise. Relief washed over her, and she gulped in air. Jeremiah edged back into the balloon, pulling her with him.

Together, they tumbled into a heap on the floor. Amelia couldn't tell which of them was shaking more. They clung to each other for a moment.

Jeremiah gasped for air. "Why the hell did you do that? You almost fell!"

The balloon jerked in a shifting wind current.

Amelia pushed his hands aside and jumped to her feet. "We'll talk later. This time, I'll get the darn cord pulled and we'll stay down. Turn around and brace your back against this side. Hang on."

The balloon hit the ground, bounced once, twice, then tipped over as the wind grabbed the deflating envelope. Amelia and Jeremiah rolled out to land unceremoniously in the dirt.

Amelia leapt up and ran to hug her parents, then traded hugs with Debbie and Alice. "We did it!"

The media people swarmed around them, all of them talking at once. Amelia raised her hands. "Please. Give us a few minutes to get ourselves together. I'll answer your questions by the trailer. Please."

The gathered crowd gave in and moved to the truck to wait.

Amelia turned back to Debbie and Alice. "Thanks, guys. We made it in one piece."

She heard a disgusted snort behind her and turned. Amelia watched Jeremiah slowly get to his feet, watched him deliberately brush the dirt from his pants, watched the storm building in him.

She tried to diffuse the explosion she saw coming. "Jeremiah Beach—my parents, Charles and Elizabeth Dedham."

Her father extended a hand to him. Jeremiah gave it a quick shake and nodded at the silver-haired man. "It's a pleasure, sir. Mrs. Dedham, would you excuse us? I need a word with your daughter."

Amelia saw the curious look that her parents exchanged. They knew her too well, and obviously understood that Jeremiah was more than just another reporter covering her story. She'd have questions to answer later, she was sure.

Without warning, he grabbed her hand and dragged

her away, shouting for the crew to handle the balloon. Assuming privacy would be a good thing, Amelia let him lead her into the edge of the forest before she jerked to a halt.

"What are you doing, Jeremiah?"

"You nearly died back there."

She shrugged. "And your point is?"

He grabbed her shoulders and snatched her close. "You could have fallen and all you can do is think of the damn record?"

"I didn't fall. I did make the record. It was very important to me." She slid the tip of her tongue around suddenly dry lips. Amelia watched pain flicker over his features. "What's the problem?"

Jeremiah groaned and captured her lips with his own. Need roared through her body like wind in the trees. Every fiber, every nerve felt raw and used, but Amelia's desire for him pushed reason aside.

Minutes later, he raised his head. "The problem is I love you too much to let you go."

"You have to. You can't go through this every time I try something new. You know that. And I don't want to wait around baking cookies while you're on assignment in the Middle East or Colombia or Africa or someplace."

"We'll find a way to make this work."

Amelia shook her head. "No, eventually we'd make each other quit the things we love best. We'd resent each other and hate each other for that. You need to go back to Phoenix, and I need to get on with what I do best."

He pulled back and ran his fingers over her forehead and across her cheek as though memorizing her features. "Can we at least have dinner? Don't make me say good-bye before I have to. I want to build more memories before it's too late."

Amelia fought for self-control. Why did the lust in her body have to equal the love in her heart? She might be able to deal with only one of them. But both . . . Amelia remembered the touch of those hands on her bare skin. Remembered his strength, his very male sensuality. Remembered . . .

What the heck? She gave in to the desire that gripped her body and tipped her mouth up to be claimed by his. When she could, she pulled away and looked directly into his eyes.

"One more night, Jeremiah. Then you go."

CHAPTER TWELVE

Amelia watched Debbie and the others pull out of the yard. Slowly, she walked into the office and pulled a bottle of her grandmother's favorite champagne from the small refrigerator. The day she'd decided to go for this record, she'd put it in to chill. Amelia popped the cork and filled a crystal flute.

In front of the picture Jeremiah had commented on, Amelia raised her glass. "To you, Grandmother. We did it. The record is yours." Amelia sipped as her eyes grew wet. "I love you," she whispered, her voice thick with unshed tears. She refused to let them spoil this day.

Amelia thought of Jeremiah, of how he had looked at the photo and then at her, wondering at the strong resemblance between her and her grandmother. Fresh pain started deep within. He'd be leaving far too soon. She trembled and decided she knew how to erase Jeremiah's image from her mind. She'd do it with a long run.

* * *

Amelia sprinted, then jogged and sprinted again until she was ready to drop. She ran her usual route—twice. Any lingering desire for Jeremiah she chased away in a frigid, mind-numbing shower.

Amelia was in control again. She would keep things cool, no seduction scene tonight. Jeremiah could eat dinner, ask her his final questions about the flight and go away.

Right. Like that's going to happen, Amelia told herself. She gritted her teeth and leaned into the refrigerator to pull out something to cook. She'd fixed him her two favorite foods, Chinese and Mexican. He'd get just plain country cooking tonight. She slammed a whole chicken down on the cutting board. And that was all he would get.

Her stomach tightened. Who would get the worst end of that deal? If she cut him off, she cut herself off. Could she resist him while they were alone—and close together? Amelia slapped her hand against her thigh. Get your mind out of the bedroom, she thought, then laughed. They hadn't made it to the bedroom, so that wasn't the problem. His being in the same house alone with her was the problem.

Amelia reached for the phone to call and cancel, but let her hand fall back to her side. She wasn't a coward. She'd face him, talk to him and have dinner with him. And that was all. With determination, she squared her shoulders and put the herb-coated bird into a pan and into the oven.

A knock on the back door stopped her mental

chewing out. She pushed the door open. Jeremiah was decked out in black, all black. Tight black jeans, slick black silk shirt. His sleeves were rolled back, revealing tanned forearms. The open neck showed off a well-muscled chest.

Primal need stole her control. Amelia wanted nothing more than to run her hands over his bare flesh, to feel him inside her. Her body longed for the sex that she desperately needed to avoid for the sake of her own sanity.

One more night won't hurt anything.

With a soft curse, she gave in to her inner voice. Amelia launched herself into his arms, laughing when he grabbed her to keep them from falling. His arms slid around her and crossed behind her back.

Her lips took his, he didn't have a choice. When his mouth opened to her, Amelia deepened the kiss and plundered. With her lips locked on his and her hands on either side of his face, Amelia carefully stepped backward, drawing him into the house.

She leaned back to look at his face and ran her fingers over his dimples. Amelia wanted nothing more at that moment than to devour every inch of his body.

"What are you smiling at?" she asked.

"You. When you make up your mind about something, you just do it. I like that." He pulled his hands from behind her back and revealed a dozen gold, orange and brown flowers. "Thought you might like these." In his other hand, he had a bottle of fine champagne.

"Thanks. That was really nice of you." Suddenly embarrassed by her blatant attack on his body, Amelia took the flowers to put into a vase. "Glasses are over there."

"I remember." His voice was low and husky. The sound shivered across her sensitive skin, raising tiny bumps on her flesh.

She watched as he unwired and popped the cork, carefully wrapping a towel over it so it wouldn't fly to the ceiling. Amelia picked up the glasses and held them for him to pour the bubbling liquid.

Finished, he saluted her with a raised glass.

"Congratulations." They clinked glasses, sipped. "I don't think I said that at the field today."

"No, you said plenty of other things, but not that."

"I'm sorry—"

"Look—"

They broke off and laughed nervously. "Let's go into the living room," Amelia said. "We'll be more comfortable there."

Jeremiah nodded and followed her into the room where they'd been the night before.

Amelia deliberately chose a chair and sank into the overstuffed teal and rose pillows. She didn't want him close enough to touch her, not yet, not while they talked.

"So, you were going to say?" she asked.

"I was going to apologize. What you choose to do is none of my business." His gaze softened as though he was lost in memories. He shuddered. "I was really afraid for you. My emotions ran away with my mouth."

"That's all right. I owe you an apology, too. I get pretty hot-tempered when people tell me what to do."

Jeremiah chuckled. "You surprise me at times."

She tipped her head to one side. "Why?"

"Oh, I don't know. You seem so . . . practical."

Amelia laughed at him.

"All right, so that's not the word I want. How about logical, analytical? I don't know. You just caught me off guard when you came at me about getting in your space. You were so ticked off by it. The only other time I'd seen that much emotion was when you talked about your grandmother, flying . . . or in front of that fireplace."

A heated flush spread from the base of her throat over her cheeks. Energy pulsed in the air between them like a living thing. Amelia twirled the crystal flute between her fingers as she focused on the champagne circling inside. That's what she felt like. Caught in an endless whirlpool with no way to escape as it sucked her under the surface.

"So what now? You go back to Phoenix or on to the Middle East or whatever, and I stay here?" Amelia sipped, tasted nothing but bubbles, and set her glass aside.

"I honestly don't know. Let's agree to disagree for the moment and see how it plays out."

Rays from the setting sun filtered through the window to backlight Jeremiah. The golden glow touched his hair and emphasized the lighter flecks in his eyes. His smile reached those eyes and happy lines spread around them.

She had seen him show every emotion in the book in the last several days. He had shared with her more than any man ever had. And he had been proud of her today. She was sure she had detected that in spite of the fear threatening to engulf them. Amelia saw in Jeremiah everything she wanted and needed in a lifelong mate.

A soft love song came on the radio playing quietly behind them. Amelia stood and looked down at her jeans, T-shirt and bare feet. "I'm not exactly dressed for this, but will you dance with me?" She lifted her hand, inviting Jeremiah to take it. She knew she was also offering herself.

He set his glass aside and put his hand in hers, letting her pull him to his feet. "You look beautiful," he whispered.

He drew her into his arms and together they swayed to the romantic music. His heart beat steadily against the cheek she laid against his chest. One hand rested against her lower back, the fingers spread across the soft curve of her bottom. He cupped her and squeezed gently, drawing her swaying hips against his own. His thigh slipped between her legs as they moved in rhythm to the melody.

Jeremiah slid his hands over her back and up to sink his fingers in her hair, using the shining mass to very gently pull her head back. He rained kisses over her eyes, her nose, her chin, then feathered his lips down the creamy curve of her neck.

Amelia moaned and stepped back. She fought the emotion that tried to stop her words. "Let's try the bed this time."

"Good idea," he said as he swung her into his arms, and crushed her against his chest. She threw her arms around his neck.

"Hey, I can't breathe," she said, laughing.

"Sorry." Jeremiah loosened his hold, but didn't set her down.

"I can walk."

He feigned a frown. "I thought this was supposed to be romantic. Isn't it working?"

"Oh, yes. It's working. Down the hall on the right."

Amelia dropped her head against his shoulder, and Jeremiah carried her away.

Amelia stretched and slid her hand over the sheets expecting to find Jeremiah. The bed was empty and the bathroom light shone under the door. He had apparently pulled a sheet and blanket over her to keep her warm when he'd crawled out of bed.

She propped up on an elbow and reached across his pillow to turn on the light. She dropped back against his side of the bed and sniffed the sheet that still held his musky scent mingled with that of love-making.

Lovemaking, not sex, she realized. She was so deeply in love with him, she'd never see the light of day. And tomorrow he'd be driving that high-powered car south, and away from her. Tears threatened, but she refused to let them fall. This was their last evening, and she wasn't going to ruin it by feeling sorry for herself. Amelia wanted every possible memory of him she could hold on to.

She heard him murmuring but couldn't make out the words. Who on earth was he talking to in the bathroom? Maybe Chuck called again, and he'd taken his cell phone in there so he wouldn't wake her.

Amelia slipped from the bed and into a heavy pink bathrobe. Winter was definitely on the way. She went into the hall to turn on the heat, and when she returned, he opened the door and walked into the room. He stopped and leaned against the wall.

"Well, you're awake."

His smile was warm, almost tender. Why did that scare her to death? Was he leaving now instead of tomorrow?

She tried to sound nonchalant. "What's up? I thought I heard you on the phone."

He looked slightly taken aback. "Oh, uh, Chuck called. That's all. I told him about you making it. He said congrats."

Amelia nodded and studied his face. What was he hiding? *Make the most of the time you have,* her inner voice said.

"Tell him thanks. How about some dinner? It smells like chicken out there."

Amelia closed the dishwasher door. "I'll run those later. Not worth the water when I cook for two."

A frown creased his forehead, and Jeremiah tossed the towel he'd used to help on the counter. "You cook for two often?"

It was asked quietly as though the answer wouldn't matter. Amelia knew it did matter to him, and was thrilled. She thought briefly of playing on his unexpected jealousy but decided against it. That wasn't her style.

"Only when I have a girlfriend over or one of my parents. When what you love to do gets you up at three in the morning, you don't have much of a social life." Amelia lifted his hand and led him into the living room. "What about you?"

"Same as you, I guess. When you have a job that takes you all over the world, it's kind of hard to date or build lasting relationships."

"Oh, look!" Amelia jumped to her feet and raced to the window, gleeful as a child.

Jeremiah stepped to her side and gazed out, then groaned.

"What? It's wonderful, the first snow of the season down here in the plains." Filigree shapes the size of nickles floated toward earth. "Isn't it beautiful? How can each one be different?"

Jeremiah gave a mock shudder, then slipped his arm around her shoulders to draw her close as he laughed with her.

"Hey, I'm sore from hitting the ground today. How about you?" she asked.

He looked at her, a flicker of suspicion in his eyes. "You'd be asking that because?"

"Have you ever used a hot tub in the snow?"

He dropped his arm from her shoulders and shuddered for real. "Snow? Remember, I'm a desert boy, and I like things hot. The hotter the better. Do I look like I'd go out in this to sit in a bubbling tub of water?"

She gave him a mischievous smile, grabbed the belt of her robe and pulled it loose. Amelia watched his eyes darken with desire as she allowed the fabric to slip from her shoulders to land at her feet. She ran the tip of her tongue around her lips and let it linger at the corner of her mouth before raising one brow at him.

"Last one in is a rotten egg." She turned and dashed for the door with Jeremiah right behind. When she glanced over her shoulder, she saw his clothes flying in all directions as he ran after her.

They leapt into the hot water, and Jeremiah gasped at the contrast of the heat with the freezing air. Snowflakes landed on his eyelashes and skin, turning his cheeks pink. Amelia drifted in the water, coming close to kiss them away. Her hand found his knee and slid up his thigh until her fingers closed over his hardness.

Jeremiah pulled her over his body and settled her there while he reverently caressed her beautiful breasts. She drifted a bit in the foaming water but came back to claim his lips with her own. Together, they sank chin deep in the water, kissing, touching and murmuring words of love.

The snow flurry had ended and the moon was out long before he lifted her from the water, wrapped her in a towel, and took her back to bed.

* * *

Amelia bolted up, slapped the ringing alarm and fell back against the pillows in total confusion. She knew she hadn't set it. Dread settled around her heart. Was he that eager to be on his way? She turned to ask him, only to find him already up and gone.

She threw aside the covers and raced for her robe. Still tying the belt at the waist, she ran from the room and straight into Jeremiah. He caught her arms and held on before they both crashed to the floor.

"Geez, you look like the devil himself is on your tail. What's up?"

"I, ah, I thought you'd gone." She sucked air into her lungs, wondering what on earth she would do when he did leave if this was what happened when she only thought he had.

He looked into her eyes. "I wouldn't do that to you, Amelia." He said her name with such tenderness that she wished with all her heart she could hear him say it that way forever.

"Good. I wanted to say good-bye." A frown fought with her smile and won. "Are you leaving already?"

"Nope."

"Then why are you up so early? I'm not flying today," Amelia said.

"Nope." He caught her arm and dragged her toward the front of the house. The sun peeked over the horizon and the prairie grasses quickly lightened. He wrapped a coat around her shoulders and stepped out onto the abobe verandah, pulling her along behind him.

"Jeremiah, what are you doing?"

"I wanted to see one more sunrise with you."

Sorrow hit her hard, very hard. "All right." She fought to keep her voice level. "Nothing quite like a Colorado sunrise over the mountains."

"Right," he agreed.

She caught the slight twitch of the corner of his mouth and wondered fleetingly what he was up to. Then her attention went skyward.

"Hey, look. Somebody's up already. Two of them."

The gigantic balloons drifted closer, one covered with rainbow colored patchwork and the other with white clouds and angels.

"Do you recognize them?"

She shook her head. "No. Must be from out of town. Lots of people come here to fly because of the view."

Jeremiah slipped one arm around her shoulders and pulled her close. "Looks to me like they have something stretched out between them. What the heck is it?"

Amelia shaded her eyes against the sun glare. "You're right. What the . . ." Then sudden tears gathered and overflowed.

Jeremiah handed her a handkerchief. "Don't turn the waterworks on, what is it?"

"It's a banner." She turned to face him. She wanted to remember how he looked. "It says, 'Marry me. I love you.' "

He kissed the tip of her nose. "Well, what's the answer?"

"Is there a method to your madness? Does the balloon proposal mean you'll work at getting used to my flying?"

He pulled her close. "It means I'll never let you go, no matter what, and yes, I'll get used to you flying if it kills me." He smiled at her. "I don't know if I want to tell you, but do you know that in Phoenix they can fly twice a day instead of just once like here?"

"Twice a day? Hmm, sounds like we might have to check it out. But what about your work? I can try, but there's no guarantee I'll ever get used to you going off on dangerous assignments."

"There are no guarantees to anything, Amelia. I'll still have to take the occasional difficult job, but how about I finally try my hand at writing the great American novel? Could you live with a novelist?"

She threw her arms around his neck, laughing against his throat. "You bet I can."

"And can you live on peanut butter and crackers while I start to build a new career?"

"Peanut butter's my favorite food. It's sweet, it's crunchy, it's—" Amelia held his face in her hands. "It's wonderful. You're wonderful. I love you."

"Is that a yes?" he asked softly.

"Yes!"

"We'll have to work at this, but I know we can do it. Together we'll reach new heights of passion, of love, even in the air if we have to."

"Passion and love in the air?"

Jeremiah laughed. "That's not exactly what I meant, but you're the pilot. Can we do that?"

Amelia threw her arms around his neck and kissed him long and lovingly. Together they could do anything.

ABOUT THE AUTHOR

Kathleen Wells is an avid romance reader and writer. Raised by an aeronautical engineer and pilot, she loves to fly and to incorporate flying into her books whenever possible. This book allowed her the opportunity to research and try hot air ballooning for the first time. She fell in love with it and can't wait to go up again!

When she isn't writing, Kathleen enjoys spending time with her husband, daughters, sons-in-law, and grandchildren. Besides spoiling the grandkids, she pampers two horses, a dog and a cat.

Readers are invited to write to Kathleen at:

P.O. Box 483
Fountain, CO 80817

Readers can also E-mail her at *DoctorW@worldnet.att.net* or visit her Web site at *www.kathleenwells.com*